BAD TURN

Fargo drew abreast of the fleeing horseman. "Pull up and you ride away alive!" Skye shouted.

The man's answer was a shot that came uncomfortably close. Fargo fired and saw the man clutch his thigh and topple from his horse, his gun flying. Fargo reined in and looked down at the figure on the ground. "Jesus, my leg," the man groaned.

"Your doing. I want some answers. Turn over," Fargo said. He saw the man start to turn and then glimpsed the second gun in his hand. The Trailsman swore as he ducked and the bullet grazed Fargo's hat. His Colt barked and the figure shuddered and lay still. "Damn fool," Fargo muttered.

Another live lead had turned into a dead end. . . .

THE
TRAILSMAN
132

KENTUCKY
COLTS

by

Jon Sharpe

A SIGNET BOOK

SIGNET
Published by the Penguin Group
Penguin Books USA Inc., 375 Hudson Street,
New York, New York 10014, U.S.A.
Penguin Books Ltd, 27 Wrights Lane,
London W8 5TZ, England
Penguin Books Australia Ltd, Ringwood,
Victoria, Australia
Penguin Books Canada Ltd, 10 Alcorn Avenue,
Toronto, Ontario, Canada M4V 3B2
Penguin Books (N.Z.) Ltd, 182-190 Wairau Road,
Auckland 10, New Zealand

Penguin Books Ltd, Registered Offices:
Harmondsworth, Middlesex, England

First published by Signet, an imprint of New American Library,
a division of Penguin Books USA Inc.

First Printing, December, 1992
10 9 8 7 6 5 4 3 2 1

Copyright © Jon Sharpe, 1992
All rights reserved

The first chapter of this book previously appeared in *Beartown Bloodshed,*
the one hundred thirty-second volume in this series.

 REGISTERED TRADEMARK—MARCA REGISTRADA

Printed in the United States of America

The Trailsman

Beginnings . . . they bend the tree and they mark the man. Skye Fargo was born when he was eighteen. Terror was his midwife, vengeance his first cry. Killing spawned Skye Fargo, ruthless, cold-blooded murder. Out of the acrid smoke of gunpowder still hanging in the air, he rose, cried out a promise never forgotten.

The Trailsman they began to call him all across the West: searcher, scout, hunter, the man who could see where others only looked, his skills for hire but not his soul, the man who lived each day to the fullest, yet trailed each tomorrow. Skye Fargo, the Trailsman, the seeker who could take the wildness of a land and the wanting of a woman and make them his own.

*Kentucky, 1860, where the
Wabash joins the Ohio, a land that
wore respectability as a mask that hid
hate, greed, twisted love,
and death . . .*

1

"You've your nerve."

"That's been said before."

"My husband's the mayor of this town."

"Hell, I know that. He sent for me."

"Then how dare you say those things to me?"

"You've been wanting me to say them, honey."

"That's nonsense."

"That's fact. You've been sending signals ever since I got here three days ago."

"You've misunderstood simple politeness."

"I'm called the Trailsman, remember? I read signs. That's my life, reading signs."

"I'm hardly a blade of grass or some prairie trail."

"A sign's a sign, a trail's a trail, grass or ass, prairie or pussy. There's not much difference."

"When the mayor gets back I'm going to tell him what you said to me and he'll send you packing."

"No you won't and no he won't."

"What makes you so sure I won't?"

"I told you, I read signs. I know teasin' from thirstin'. I can tell playin' from pantin'."

"I don't have to wait for my husband to get back. When he's away I'm the acting mayor."

"No shit."

"That's right. That's how the town charter reads. I can have you thrown out of town right now.

"On what charge?"

"I'll think of something. Disorderly conduct. That'll do."

"Honey, I haven't started being disorderly."

The big man with the handsomely chiseled face stepped back, but his lake blue eyes stayed on the woman in front of him. Libby Bradbury was still on the sunny side of forty, about five feet five inches tall with a slightly overdone, earthy body she emphasized with tight outfits and low-cut necklines that showed the cleavage of deep breasts. Blond hair that kept its blondness with the help of a bottle just avoided looking brassy. Worn short, it framed a compact face, still attractive with enough roundness to it to push away the tiny wrinkles of time. Full lips, a small nose, and dark brown eyes that seemed to hold a perpetual smolder completed the picture.

"You leave this house at once, Mister Fargo," Libby Bradbury said, drawing indignation around her.

"Just what I was going to do," Skye Fargo said. "But I'll be back tomorrow night. I'm feeling kindly."

"Kindly?"

"Yes. I'll give you one more chance to do what you want to do."

"You'll be wasting your time," she snapped.

"Tell me not to come," he challenged and saw Libby Bradbury's eyes grow smaller and her tongue slide across her full lips for an instant. Then she lifted her chin and met the mocking smile in his eyes with bold defiance.

"Don't come," she said and he shrugged and started to turn to the front door of the house. "Are you convinced now?" she tossed at him.

"Are you?" He laughed as he pulled the door open and stepped outside into the night. The woman came to the doorway and watched him pull himself into the saddle, and he saw the light from inside the house outline the curves of her full-hipped figure. Her voice came to him, her tone carefully correct and aloof.

"Of course, you can come by tomorrow night to see if the mayor's come back," she said. "That'd be different."

He let his smile answer and she spun on her heel and slammed the door shut. The smile stayed with him as he put the magnificent Ovaro into a slow walk through the dark streets of the town. Libby Bradbury had been only one of the surprises he'd had since arriving in town. But she certainly had been the pleasantest and most intriguing. She had tossed a lot of questions at him when he'd arrived to see Sam Bradbury, none of which he could answer and he'd first thought her signals had been just window dressing to get answers. But he had seen that tried often enough and he knew the difference. Libby Bradbury was both actively curious and actively smoldering.

The town itself had been another surprise. It was much more respectable than he'd expected with a bank, a hotel, a proper meeting hall, a number of white-fenced homes, and a thorough assortment of shops from a barber to a blacksmith. But he realized he shouldn't have expected a frontier town. This part of Kentucky where it bordered on Missouri was no longer what it was when Daniel Boone, John Sevier, and Jim Robertson had opened the land. Few families came down Boone's Trace any longer, and the old Kentucky cabins with their Piedmont heritage were hardly seen anymore, nor were the old splint brooms and home wool cards for weaving. Men no longer staked their claims by marking "witness trees" with axe marks. Land was registered properly now.

Yet that had all been less than seventy years back, and while most of the big game was gone, Kentucky was still a rich and fertile land. While the old wild farms had given way to proper plantation farming and horse-breeding land, its heritage was still in the land and its people. Respectability wasn't ever much of a thick cloak and in places here it was but a thin veneer. Yet it didn't seem the kind of town or land that would need the talents of a Trailsman, and Fargo still wondered about the note that had brought him here as he walked the Ovaro down the dark night streets toward the yellow glow of light a little past the center of town. The sounds of voices, laughter and the clinking of glasses, drifted into the night with the yellow glow as he reached the saloon, dismounted, and tethered the horse at the hitching post.

The somewhat elegant name of the town, Windsor Bell, had been echoed in the sign over the swinging doors to the saloon. BELL'S BELLES, it proclaimed in faded gold lettering, and he pushed his way through the doors. This made his third night's visit to the saloon since he'd arrived, but he was still very much the stranger and regarded as such by the regulars. The long bar took up one side of the room, tables along the other and girls in black stockings and abbreviated outfits tended to the customers, all of them with faces too cynical too soon. Perhaps the town wore respectability, but the saloon was little different than any other anywhere. The one end of the bar was relatively uncrowded and he stepped to the wooden rail.

"Bourbon," he said. "No bar slop, please." The bartender brought a bottle from under the counter and set it in front of him with a shot glass. Fargo started to reach for the bottle when two men stepped to the bar, one at each side of him, and suddenly he felt others pressing up behind him. He started to turn when he felt the Colt jerked from his holster and he spun to see three men back away, one stuffing the Colt into his pocket. The two men at each side also stepped back and Fargo's eyes narrowed at the man who'd taken his Colt, a tall but thin figure with an unkempt mustache. "I'd give that back, mister," Fargo growled.

"You can have it after we see you out of town," the man said. "We don't want anybody gettin' shot."

"You're not seeing anybody out of town either, so give it back," Fargo said. The man wore a loose calf-skin jacket over the top part of his thin frame and the Colt made a bulge in his pocket.

"Just come along and there'll be no trouble," the man said. Fargo's eyes swept the other four. All ordinary cowhand types, one in a tan Stetson wearing nervousness in his face. But he wasn't about to let them have their way in some isolated spot.

"Wrong again. There's going to be trouble," Fargo said.

The thin one muttered out of the side of his mouth to the others. "Get him," he said and they started forward. Fargo's hand shot out, closed around the bottle on the bar and he swung it in a backhand sweep and felt it smash against the side of a face.

"Oh, Jesus," the voice cried out as Fargo turned, saw the man fall backward, one hand clutched to the side of his head. The others had paused for a moment but now came at him again and Fargo, clutching the neck of the broken bottle in his hand, ducked a swinging right and brought the jagged bottle upward. The sharp glass sliced into the armpit of one of his attackers and the man screamed in pain as he twisted and fell stumbling away.

"Get the sheriff and the mayor," Fargo heard the bartender call out as he twisted away from the three figures that rushed at him. He turned and glimpsed one of the three leap at him from the rear and braced himself as the man landed on his back. Throwing the piece of bottle away to avoid falling on it, he let himself go forward, dropped to his knees and tossed the man over his head. He dove to one side as a kick missed his head, the screams of the girls filling the background, rolled across the floor to come up at a table. He came to his knees, saw four of the five figures charging at him, one with the side of his face streaming red.

Fargo half rose, spun, and upended the round table as the thin figure and another man reached him. He used the table as a battering ram, putting all the strength of his leg muscles behind it as he smashed it into the two men. They went backward as he pushed forward and one stumbled, went to one knee. Fargo rose from behind the table swinging a long, looping left that had lost a little of its power when he caught the tall, thin one on the point of the jaw. The man staggered backward and dropped to one knee and Fargo saw the one with the bloodstained face diving at him across the table, his arms outstretched, his mouth twisted in fury and pain. Fargo stepped back and pulled the table with him and the man fell forward, off balance. Fargo's left hook and following right landed flush on his jaw and he flew backward, twisting in a half-circle before he hit the floor.

The other two came around the table and charged at him, arms swinging blows. They were bumping into each other in their rush to get at him and Fargo sidestepped, sank a hard left into the nearest one's midsection and the man grunted as he doubled up. The other one shifted and rushed again. Fargo ducked his wild, roundhouse blows and lifted a tremendous uppercut that landed with all the strength of his upper arm behind it. The man almost jackknifed backward as he flew through the air and landed on the floor. The other had regained enough breath to attack again, and Fargo easily blocked his amateurish blows, ducked under a particularly wild swing, seized his arm, twisted and flung the man halfway across the room. His somewhat paunchy figure slammed into the bar where he hung for a moment and then slithered to the floor to lay half against the brass footrest.

Fargo spun as he heard the sound just to his right and saw that the thin one had recovered enough to try again. He ducked away from a downward punch, blocked a follow-through left and sank his own right deep into the man's abdomen. As the thin figure doubled over, Fargo brought his knee up hard into the man's face. The man's head snapped back as he sailed through the air and landed spread-eagled on the floor. Fargo drew himself erect and his eyes scanned the scene. His five assailants were unconscious in various positions and spread across the barroom floor, almost from one side to the other, ending with the paunchy figure lying against the base of the bar. The girls and a number of the customers were crowded against the walls, looking on now in awed silence.

Fargo stepped to the thin man and retrieved his Colt just as Libby Bradbury strode in with a slightly built, gray-haired man with a tired face and a sheriff's badge attached to his shirt. Libby Bradbury wore an outer coat wrapped around herself, and she halted to stare wide-eyed at the scene. She looked up as Fargo paused beside her. "Now that's disorderly conduct, honey," he said as he walked from the bar. Outside he swung onto the Ovaro and rode slowly away from the saloon. The attack had been just one more thing in what was becoming a list of surprises, and he rode the pinto up into the low hills, found a stand of honey locust and made a small fire to warm up some of the beef jerky from his saddlebag. When he finished eating he sat back and let the fire burn itself out as his thoughts turned backward, first to the letter that had brought him to Windsor Bell and then to but a few days ago when he'd neared the town.

The letter had come to him general delivery in Kansas where he had delivered a herd of cattle across a new trail for the Clemson Brothers. The letter nestled inside his shirt pocket and he'd no need to read it again, the words firm inside his mind:

> Bill Bowlder and the Clemson Brothers have told me that you're the very best and I've a job for the very best trailsman there is. The enclosed cash is just a down payment and traveling money. I'll be waiting to see you soon as you can get here.
>
> Sam Bradbury, Mayor
> Windsor Bell, Kentucky

The down payment had been more than he got on most jobs, not the kind of money to turn down. Besides, he'd no other jobs waiting and so he'd pocketed the cash and taken the high trail east through that tinderbox divided state, Missouri, spent a few nights in St. Louis, and then moved into Indiana and turned south into the Kentucky land.

He had been moving along a roadway bordered by low hills and heavy growths of bitternut and sycamore when he met Barnaby Olsen. The figure on the sturdy-rumped gray mare blocked his way along the road, thick white hair and a beard to match and a dark brown buckskin jacket. Fargo drew to a halt and met the man's sharp, clear gaze fastened on him with crackling blue eyes. " 'Afternoon, traveler," the man said and Fargo guessed him to be pushing seventy but his figure ramrod straight. He wore an old Massachusetts Arms revolver, Fargo noted, a six-shot single-action gun with a gear-rotated cylinder that fired a .32 bullet, no gun for fast shooting but steady and accurate enough.

" 'Afternoon.'' Fargo nodded. The white-haired man didn't move his gray mare but Fargo saw his eyes take him in with narrow-eyed appraisal. "Something I can do for you, old-timer?'' Fargo asked pleasantly.

"No, sonny,'' the man answered and Fargo smiled at the rejoinder. "But maybe there's something I can do for you,'' the man added.

"Never refuse a favor,'' Fargo said.

"Would you be on your way to Windsor Bell?'' the old man asked.

"I would,'' Fargo answered.

"Figured so,'' the man said. "This is the only road to Windsor Bell coming down north. By the way, the name's Barnaby . . . Barnaby Olsen.''

"Fargo . . . Skye Fargo. Now, what was it you can do for me?''

"Depends on if you're the right one,'' Barnaby Olsen said.

"You always talk in circles?'' Fargo smiled.

"Only when things don't seem to run straight, such as now, for instance,'' the old man said. "There are four fellers up the road a piece waiting to drygulch somebody.''

Fargo felt his brows lift. "What makes you sure they're waiting to drygulch somebody?'' he asked.

"What makes you know when a cougar's ready to pounce?'' Barnaby Olsen said, and Fargo smiled at the way the old-timer could snap out answers. "Besides, they've been waiting for the past three days,'' Barnaby added.

"How'd you come to spot them?'' Fargo queried.

"There's a deer trail higher in the hills. I usually take it when I'm out alone, which is pretty near all the time. I like it. Gives a nice view of the land. I was on it when I spotted them a few days ago, then saw them again when I passed the next two days. I decided to hang around and watch."

"You know these four?" Fargo asked.

"Never saw them before. A good number of riders and wagons have taken the road past them, most of 'em folks from around here and they went through without trouble. I got the feeling they were waiting for somebody different. When I saw you coming along, the first stranger I saw on the road, I decided to come down and stop you."

"I'm much obliged to you, Barnaby," Fargo said.

"You know why there'd be drygulchers waiting for you?" the old man asked.

"No. Leastwise not yet. If they are waiting for me," Fargo said.

"Yes, *if* they are," Barnaby conceded. "What brings you to these parts, Fargo?"

"Mayor Sam Bradbury sent for me," Fargo told him. "Don't even know why, yet."

Barnaby Olsen lifted one white eyebrow. "I'd heard he'd sent for somebody," the man said. "There's been a heap of trouble lately."

"You want to tell me about it?" Fargo suggested.

"Sam Bradbury hired you. I figure the tellin's for him to do," Barnaby said.

"Fair enough," Fargo agreed. "You want to tell me where these four men are hiding?"

"You keep on along the road and you'll pass a twisted bitternut that bends almost half around itself. There's a curve after that. They're just on the other side of the curve."

"Then I'd best be getting on," Fargo said.

Barnaby Olsen's white eyebrows lowered in a

frown. "You going to ride right into an ambush after I've told you about it?"

"How else will I know if it's me they're after?" Fargo said with a broad grin at the disapproval on Barnaby's crinkly face.

"Seems a hell of a hard way to find out," the old man muttered.

"You coming along?" Fargo asked blandly.

"Hell, no. One damfool's enough," Barnaby snapped.

"You're not curious?"

"Sure I'm curious but I'll be curious from up on my deer trail, which you ought to take and pass them by," Barnaby said.

"I'd like to find out if I'm their target," Fargo said. "Thanks again for the warning, my friend. I won't forget it."

"Good luck to you," Barnaby said, disapproval still in his face as he turned the sturdy gray mare and disappeared into the sycamores that climbed upward.

Fargo sent the Ovaro forward at a slow walk as thoughts danced through his head. If he could rig up a dummy and they poured bullets into it, it'd fall and they'd see it for what it was. But he'd have the answer he wanted, he pondered and his lips drew back in a grimace. He didn't have the time or the materials to make a proper dummy, even one with the hat pulled down low, not one good enough to pass for real in the daylight. They'd see it as a dummy and he'd not get any answer at all. Getting an answer was important. It'd tell him enough to ride with his guard up in Windsor Bell and perhaps something about the nature of the job he'd been hired to do.

He continued to walk the Ovaro, its glistening jet black fore- and hindquarters a stark contrast to the pure white midsection. The magnificent horse he rode had often marked him, and it had possibly done so again, all of which meant that his arrival was a poorly kept secret at best. He saw the twisted bitternut come into sight, and beyond it the curve in the road, and he prodded his thoughts as he came to a halt beside the tree. He'd make use of that most perennial of human characteristics, curiosity. If they were indeed waiting for a lone rider on an Ovaro, human nature would govern their response. He'd have his answer and all he needed to turn ambushers into ambushed.

He dismounted and led the Ovaro into the curve of the road, paused to take the big Sharps rifle from its saddle holster and then, halfway through the curve, he gave the horse a smart slap on its powerful, jet black rump. The Ovaro pranced forward for a moment, slowed, and kept going at a walk. The horse would go on for another dozen yards or so before halting he knew, and he followed it around the curve and at the end of the curving path he swung to the edge and dropped to one knee. He had a clear view of the road ahead as it straightened, and he saw the Ovaro continuing to walk on for another two dozen yards before halting. Fargo stayed on one knee, the rifle raised as he scanned the thick tree growth that climbed upward on both sides of the road. He waited, silent as a mountain lion watching its prey. The Ovaro stood still, swishing its tail idly, and Fargo counted off the seconds that turned into minutes.

A grim smile touched his lips as he finally saw the movement in the trees to the right side of the road, branches moving, a trail of quivering leaves marking a figure moving down to the road. Two figures he corrected himself, as he saw the two men step onto the road, both with rifles in their hands, both peering down to the curve. Fargo leaned deeper into the trees and the two figures returned their eyes to the Ovaro.

"That's gotta be the horse," one man said. "See if there's any blood on the saddle. Somethin' must've happened to him." The second man strode to the Ovaro, examined the saddle seat, the cantle, and the skirt.

"Nothin' wrong here," he said and Fargo's eyes went to the other side of the road where a third figure came out of the trees. That left one more still in the tree cover he took note.

"Somethin' wrong somewhere," one of the other men said. "Let's go down the road and see."

Fargo grimaced. He'd wanted all four out where he could see them but he couldn't wait for them to come onto him. He brought the big Sharps up to his shoulder, drew a bead on one of the three figures starting toward the curve, and cursed silently. He'd never been one for shooting ducks. Everybody deserved a chance. Most always. "Drop your guns," he called out, his finger resting on the trigger. The three figures halted and then behaved as he'd been almost certain they would. One brought up his rifle to fire, and the other two dived for cover. Fargo's finger pressed the trigger and the Sharps barked. The man quivered before he could shoot, staggered in place, and collapsed. But Fargo had already swung the rifle to his left and the shot caught the man just as he started to dive into the trees. Only his head landed in the tree cover as the rest of him twisted and shuddered as the heavy slug tore through the base of his spine. But the third one had reached the trees, and Fargo ducked low as two shots tore through the leaves over his head. He flung himself sideways as another pair of bullets came closer.

The man was into the trees on the same side of the road as he was. That left the fourth bushwhacker in the tree cover on the other side. He could run, stay there, or try to cross the road. In any event he was out of the way for the moment. Fargo moved behind a tree trunk, concentrating his focus on the man somewhere near. He stayed still, listening, and the sudden trampling of brush came from almost directly in front of him. He cursed as he dropped to his knees and heard the bullet slam into the tree trunk where his head had been. He rolled, came up on his stomach, and heard the shooter moving away. The man had caught a clear glimpse of him against the tree. He'd have had his quarry if he'd known how to move silently. Fargo thanked his luck for large favors.

He rose, the ambusher making his way up the hillside through the trees, and Fargo brought himself into a low crouch as he ran, moving through the trees with the speed and silence of a gray wolf. The ambusher was making enough noise for the both of them, and Fargo slowed as he drew almost opposite the man. The drygulcher was more anxious about time and distance than silence. A mistake Fargo grunted as he shifted direction, drew closer, and glimpsed the figure darting through the trees. The man had stopped climbing and turned in a half circle Fargo saw. He had slowed also, coming up short on breath. He was clearly visible but still darting through trees, and Fargo abandoned his own silent steps and brought the big Sharps up as he ran crashing through the brush.

The ambusher heard him and turned instantly. He came to a halt, started to bring his own rifle up, exactly as Fargo expected he would. The ambusher only had his rifle half upraised when the shot tore through his chest. He flew backward, crashed into a tree trunk, shuddered there for a moment, and then slowly slid lifelessly to the ground. Fargo lowered the Sharps and started to move toward the man when the shot rang out. He instinctively ducked as he whirled and saw the figure that had been a little higher and behind him. The man dropped the rifle as he pitched forward onto his face, and Fargo looked up the hillside to see the thatch of white hair move down the hillside.

"He was about to split your back in half," Barnaby said, the heavy pistol still in his hand.

Fargo drew a long breath. Only one of the ambushers had been on the hill at the other side of the road. He had made a wrong assumption and it had almost been a fatal mistake. "I'm doubly obliged to you now," he said as Barnaby halted beside the lifeless figure and Fargo waited. "Know him?" he asked.

"Nope," Barnaby said and walked to the other ambusher with Fargo. "Never saw him, either." The words were echoed as he walked down to the other two on the road with Fargo. "Hired guns," Barnaby said. "Not very good ones, either."

Fargo grunted agreement as he searched the pockets of both men and found nothing to identify them. "They've got their horses just on a ways. I'll take them back to my place until tomorrow," Barnaby said. "Then I'll sell them to Harry Ekins. He's got a small corral of cowpoke ponies he sells."

"Fine with me," Fargo said as he walked to where the Ovaro waited.

"You can go your way now," the old-timer said, a note of satisfaction in his voice. "You've got your answer. They were sure waiting for you." He paused and a sudden smile creased the crinkly face. "I was wondering what you were going to do. I didn't figure you'd ride into an ambush."

"Curiosity killed the cat, remember?"

"Four polecats in this case," Barnaby said.

"If I wanted to look up Barnaby Olsen again, where would I find him?" Fargo asked.

"Take the road west from town. You'll come to an

23

old shack I've spent two years fixing up," Barnaby said.

"I'll be visiting," Fargo said. "And thanks again." Barnaby Olsen had nodded gravely and Fargo had ridden on to the respectable town of Windsor Bell.

He shut off thoughts and brought his mind back to the moment as the fire burned itself out and the night darkness closed around him. The ambush had been three days ago and tonight the attack on the bar. Somebody was very unhappy about his arrival and he hadn't any idea why. All he knew was that the man who'd sent for him was still away, and his wife still full of questions and smoldering sensuality.

Maybe he'd have at least one answer by tomorrow night he mused, as he shed clothes and drew sleep around himself.

2

The warmth of the morning sun woke him. He found a stream for washing and a cluster of wild plums for breakfasting. He decided to get the feel of the surrounding land. It could come in handy in unexpected ways. Some of it he had already seen—built-up land with an air of civilization. Yet these hills where he finished the last plum were still wild enough, thickly grown with sycamore, shagbark hickory, red mulberry and box elder. The hills themselves rose sharply in place, offering a wall of green brush bordered at the bottom by the brilliant red-orange of butterfly weed.

But he wanted more than the feel of the land, he realized. He wanted the nature of the people and he decided to pay a visit to Barnaby Olsen. He rode out of the low hills, skirted the town, and found the road that led west from it. He'd gone about a mile when he spotted the shack, boxy in shape yet sporting fresh paint, no windows hanging loose, a good, solid feel to it with a small corral in the back.

The front door opened as he reined to a halt and swung from the horse. "Been wondering when you'd come by," Barnaby Olsen said.

"Thought I'd look over the countryside," Fargo said.

The old-timer's eyes flashed quiet amusement. "Want a guide, do you?" He chuckled.

"It might help, unless you're busy," Fargo said.

"Haven't been busy in years, young feller," Barnaby said. "I'll get my gear." He reappeared in moments carrying his saddle and marched around the shack to the rear. Fargo waited in the doorway and saw that the shack was roomier than it seemed from the outside. Most of it was a large room with hide covering on the floor and snowshoes and snow poles fastened to the walls. A solid, iron Franklin stove rested against one wall and a curtained section, partly open, revealed a cot and night table.

When Barnaby came around the shack astride the gray mare, Fargo pulled himself onto the Ovaro. "Any special way?" Barnaby asked.

"East. I saw benches, banners, and a grandstand being set up in a big field yesterday. I'm curious," Fargo said.

"They're getting ready for the Windsor Bell fair. They hold it every year, goes for three days. It includes all kinds of contests, a steeplechase race, and a hoedown and barbecue. It's a right festive occasion. Some folks come from as far away as Bardstown and from across the Wabash," Barnaby said. "Starts day after tomorrow, I think."

"I might pay a visit," Fargo said. "If I'm still alive." At Barnaby's questioning glance he quickly told of the attack in the bar and Barnaby's lips were pursed when he finished.

"You're right unpopular without having earned it yet," the old-timer observed.

"My thinking exactly," Fargo agreed and followed Barnaby up into the low hills and then a little higher until he halted at a spot that afforded a long, sweeping view of the land below. Fargo saw well-tended horse farms with freshly painted fences, horses inside roomy corrals. In the distance he saw a vast field of cotton. His glance roamed the land and saw some smaller farms, but also well kept, and to his far right, what appeared to be a mining operation on a round-topped hill. He counted at least ten horse farms of various sizes as he frowned. It certainly didn't seem land that needed a trailsman. A series of hills rose up along the right side of the flat terrain, passages cutting into the hillsides. "What's on the other side?" he asked.

"The valley folks," Barnaby said and led the way along a winding path that crossed the hills horizontally until once more he halted at an outcrop and looked down, this time into a shallow, broad valley. Houses dotted the valley, almost at the edge where box elder grew heavily. But these were smaller houses, some almost ramshackle and unpainted zigzag fences along with some posthole and stump fences. He saw hogs, chickens, sheep, cows, and some horses but all in all, the valley seemed a run-down place compared with the large spreads on the other side of the hills.

"Anything to tell me?" he slid at Barnaby.

"Nope," Barnaby said.

"The valley folks are very different from the others," Fargo tried.

"By different you mean poor?" Barnaby returned. "They are, most of them clawing and struggling to stay alive."

Fargo moved the Ovaro slowly along the hills and saw the foliage was sparser, the tree growth smaller, the slopes very different from the thickly grown, wild hills that separated the valley from the wealthier, cultivated plateau. It was almost as if nature echoed man's condition and he finally turned when the sun reached mid-afternoon. "Let's head back," he said and Barnaby swung the mare alongside him. "Were you ever one of the valley folk?" Fargo asked.

"What makes you say that?" the old man answered.

"Thought I detected a note of sympathy in your voice when we spoke about them earlier," Fargo said.

"You're good, Fargo. You don't miss much," Barnaby said. "But no, I've never been one of the valley folks."

"What brought you here to that shack of yours?" Fargo questioned.

"Got tired of wandering. I'm a carpenter by trade, used to help build and repair houses all over Missouri and Indiana. Did it here in Kentucky until I quit about two years back. Oh, once in a while I still do an odd job for somebody."

"Anything else you want to tell me about Windsor Bell?" Fargo asked.

"You do your talkin' to Sam Bradbury first," Barnaby said and Fargo lapsed into silence, certain that Barnaby Olsen couldn't be pushed or tricked into talking until he was ready. The day was nearing an end when they pushed through the rugged hills that bordered the south end of the land below, and he again scanned the farms and watched a small herd of horses being chased into a stable. He was too far away to tell anything about the animals except that by their movements they were high-spirited, quality stock.

The night had descended when they reached Barnaby's shack. "Want to come in for a drink?" Barnaby asked.

"Next time," Fargo said. "If the mayor's back I'll be having my talk with him." Barnaby waved back as he rode on and Fargo sent the pinto along the pathway that led to Windsor Bell. The town was dark and closed when he reached it, except for that murmur and yellow glow that marked the saloon, and he rode past the swinging doors to the house at the north end of town. The door was quickly opened at his knock and Libby Bradbury faced him, her eyes appraising, a floor-length housedress of rosy pink that buttoned down the front almost hiding the curves of her figure. "The mayor get back?" Fargo said as he stepped in.

"No," Libby said as she closed the door and he followed her into a living room with a couch, a table, a stuffed chair, and a thick bearskin rug across the center of the floor. "I want to talk to you," she said.

"That's better," he commented.

"About that incident at the saloon last night," she said crisply.

"Too bad," he said.

"Did you know any of those men?" she asked.

"Nope. Did you?"

"No. It seems they were strangers in town."

"They didn't pop up by themselves. Somebody pointed them at me," Fargo said. "Where are they now?"

"We told them to leave town or find themselves in jail," Libby said. "Naturally, they left."

"Still want to arrest me for disorderly conduct? You've a reason now," Fargo said.

"I should have last night," Libby answered. "But the moment's gone."

Fargo took a step closer to her. "That's the trouble with moments. They're gone if you don't grab them while you can," he said and her eyes smoldered back. "Your husband ought to be back by tomorrow. That'll make another moment gone," he said.

She didn't answer but he heard the shallow sound of her breathing, suddenly quickened. His finger pulled open the top button of the housedress, did the same with the second, then the third. Libby Bradbury's eyes stayed locked on his, her full lips parted ever so slightly. "Do you intend to stop?" she asked in a breathy whisper.

"Not unless you tell me to," Fargo said.

His hand rested on the fourth button as he waited an extra twenty seconds and there was still no reply. He smiled as he flipped the button open and the soft swell of her breasts pushed up and out. He never had a chance to touch the next button as her hand came up, pulled at the housedress and half the remaining buttons flew open. Libby Bradbury wriggled her shoulders; the garment fell away and she stepped out of it, naked before him. He took in skin that was soft white, rounded shoulders, and full curved breasts with large, deep pink areolas, each centered by a pink tip. A slightly barrel chest with good spring of rib curved down to a convex little belly, and below it, a black, dense triangle. Full-fleshed thighs just avoided heaviness by sturdy muscle tone, and all of her exuding an earthy sensuousness.

Her arms lifted, slid around his neck, and her mouth came to his, lips already parted, pressing hard, moving against his and her tongue slid forward, circled into his mouth and he felt her hands helping him shed clothes. He dropped the gunbelt, tossed it to the couch, and pulled off Levi's as she drew his shirt from him. She stepped back a pace, her eyes moving hungrily over his muscled smoothness, and then her hands pressed against his chest, slid downward across his pectorals, over the trim flatness of his abdomen, down farther and suddenly she was gasping, pulling him with her down onto the bearskin rug.

"Oh, Jesus," Libby Bradbury cried out as her hands curled around his throbbing, pulsating maleness, and she held him as she pulled her breasts to press against his face. He found one deep, full mound and drew the deep pink nipple into his mouth, drew in deeper and let it rest against the back of his tongue as his hand explored the dense, black triangle, her pubic mound surprisingly soft. But then all of Libby Bradbury was soft, the extra layer of fleshiness spread evenly throughout her body. As his hand slid lower, came between her thighs and felt her skin already damp, her legs moved apart. "Christ, yes, oh, Jesus, yes," Libby bit out, her voice low and throaty, and she lifted her fleshy little belly, the dense nap pressing against him. "Yes, yes, yes . . . God, yes," she demanded and her torso was shaking in anticipation and wanting as he was still poised at the threshhold.

When he let himself enter the warm moistness of her she shouted out, almost a laugh of pleasure, and her soft thighs were locked around him at once. Libby pushed upward, her dense triangle coming against him, exciting in its touch, and she thrust upward again and then again. "Damn, oh, damn," she breathed and her thighs jiggled tight against his hips. Libby Bradbury wanted no slow lovemaking, no enticements, no subtlety. She thirsted and thrusted with an almost desperate desire, little grunting sounds spaced in between her half-screams of delight. "Yes, yes, oh, Jesus, more, more . . ." she demanded and he found himself matching her every eager prodding, his own hunger spiraling as she swept him along with her almost animal-like fury.

But suddenly the grunting broke off and Libby Bradbury's earthy body arched upward, matching the scream that arched from her to fill the room. Her thighs tightened around him and she became almost rigid save for the deep breasts that quivered and shook as her climax swept through her. Her scream paused for a split second, came again, paused and came again, and he felt her inner contractions around him echo the shrieks. He heard his own groan of pleasure as explosions commingled with inner claspings and finally, with a cry of despair, she sank down onto the rug, pulling him with her, her thighs still firmly hold-

31

ing him. She turned, rolled him onto his back and stayed around and atop him as her mouth pressed wet warmth against his and her breasts were pillowy mounds across his chest. She moved slowly, up and down against him, drawing the last remnants of ecstasy to herself, each breath a long, soft sigh until finally she unclasped her legs from around him and fell limply aside. "Jesus . . ." she whispered as she pulled his face against the deep breasts.

Fargo enjoyed the sensuousness of her full-fleshed body as he lay beside her, one hand curling around a deep-cupped breast. "Still want to arrest me?" he asked.

"Can't think of a charge," she said.

"Disturbing the piece, spelled p-i-e-c-e," he offered blandly.

Libby Bradbury rose up on one elbow. "You sure did that, Fargo," she murmured.

He studied her for a moment. "You work up quite a head of steam. I'm wondering if the mayor went away to rest."

A small, wry sound escaped her. "The mayor doesn't get and he doesn't give," she said, and Fargo lifted one eyebrow. "Ever since he was sick some while back the only riding he can do is in a carriage."

"Sorry," Fargo remarked and she shrugged and lay down across his chest. She was lying tight against him when the door opened and Fargo sat up, startled, as Libby turned on her side to stare at the doorway with him. He found himself looking at a young woman who stared back out of a handsome face, now wreathed in shock and surprise. He took in a straight nose, light blue eyes that shot blue fire at him, a sharply etched mouth, and dark brown hair worn loose and shoulder length. A light blue blouse that matched her eyes rested on breasts perhaps a little long but part of a willow-wand figure, long, lean legs encased in jeans, a horsewoman's figure. Fargo saw the young woman's eyes bore into Libby.

"Bitch. Rotten, stinking bitch," the young woman bit out.

"Get out of here," Libby said. "Next time knock before you come in."

"Two-timing slut," the young woman said, swung her eyes to Fargo and took in his muscled frame as he sat up straight. "Bastard. Enjoy yourself. It'll be your last time," she flung at him, spun on her heel, and stalked from the house, slamming the door behind with such force that a small, framed picture fell from this wall.

"Who was that?" Fargo frowned.

"A little bitch who's always where she shouldn't be. Forget her," Libby snapped, her voice hard as she sat up and began to slip into the housedress. Fargo rose, pulled on clothes, and when he finished, the woman's arms were around him again. "Feeling pleased with yourself?" she asked.

"About what?"

"About being right," Libby said.

"Never had any doubts," Fargo said.

"It was too good to do only once," she said.

"What happens when the mayor gets back?" he questioned.

"I'll find a way," she said.

"You want to tell me who our little visitor was?" he asked.

"I told you, nobody you need care about," the woman said and pressed her mouth to his. "Till next time," she murmured as he stepped back and walked to the door. Libby Bradbury wore a smug little smile, he saw, as he left. Outside he climbed onto the Ovaro and rode into the low hills where he bedded down under a red ash. The night stayed warm and he undressed to underdrawers and lay atop the bedroll, the Colt against his side. The night had been the only pleasurable moment since he'd arrived, and he was wondering if his stay in Windsor Bell would come to a quick end. He was never one to tread in a quagmire, and Windsor Bell seemed to be just that with all kinds of under-the-surface treacherousness. He closed his eyes and slept with thoughts of Libby Bradbury still clinging to him.

He let himself sleep a little longer than usual and the sun was fully over the hills when he rose, stretched, and had just drawn on trousers when the shot exploded. The spray of dirt flew up only inches from him as the bullet struck, and he flung himself sideways as another shot barely missed his diving form. He hit the ground, rolled behind a red ash and ducked again as another shot slammed into the base of the tree and sent up splinters of wood. Fargo's lake blue eyes were cold as a January lake as he scanned the hillside. The shots had come from a cluster of sycamore just below him on the hillside. Rifle fire, he grunted. But only one assailant this time, the sound of each shot the same. He flung a glance at the Ovaro and swore silently. He wanted to reach the big Sharps in the saddlecase but the horse was too far away.

Yet he had to give it a try. Maybe his attacker had taken off after his first attempt. Staying in a crouch, Fargo edged around the tree trunk and started toward the horse. The shot cracked out but two seconds after he left the tree, and he dove backward. "Damn," he swore, rolled and came up on one knee to peer down the hillside again. His attacker was still very much in place with the deadly advantage of both cover and range. Moreover, though the shooter was a fraction slow in reaction time, every bullet had come dangerously close. The attacker was a better than average shot.

Fargo frowned as his thoughts tumbled over one another. It was time to turn to the wild creatures. Each and every one had their own ways to foil an attacker. This was a moment to borrow from the 'possum's tricks, Fargo decided. His eyes measured the distance to the nearest tree. He'd only be in the open about six seconds. Maybe he could cut that to three. He rose, poised himself on one knee as a runner prepares for the starting gun. Using all the strength of powerful calf and thigh muscles, he bolted from behind the tree. He was more than halfway to the next tree and flung himself into a dive when the shot rang out.

He felt it graze his back but he cried out, a guttural cry as he disappeared behind the tree. He lay motionless, one leg extended into the clear beyond the tree, his face turned so that his cheek rested on the leaves, his eyes closed. He stayed that way, one arm outspread, breathing soft, tiny breaths. It took longer than he'd expected. His attacker was cautious. But finally Fargo's wild-creature hearing caught the sound of soft, careful footsteps. He held his breath while he opened his eyes but a fraction, just enough to see the ground as he lay motionless. The feet came into his view, then the bottom of the Levi's. He remained unmoving, still holding his breath and the legs bent, the figure coming down to peer more closely at him. He saw the muzzle of the rifle, held downward at the ground. Tensing every muscle as he held the last of his breath, he exploded, lashing out with his arm, slamming it into the ankles of the figure as he rolled and leaped, his other hand closing around the barrel of the rifle.

He yanked and it came free and his shoulder barreled into the figure, and then he whirled, swinging the rifle around to fire at the figure on the ground. He halted, felt the frown dig into his brow as he saw the dark brown, shoulder-length hair, the light blue eyes looking up at him and a lovely mouth parted, still gulping in air. "You, goddammit," he growled. The young woman blinked, pushed herself onto both elbows, and glowered up at him.

"That's right," she said, the light blue eyes crackling.

"Get up," he ordered and she pushed to her feet, drew her long, willowy figure up straight, no contrition in her handsome face, he noted. "Who the hell are you?" Fargo barked.

"Karen Bradbury," she snapped and knew she saw the surprise come into his face. "Sam Bradbury is my father," she added icily.

Fargo let thoughts arrange themselves for a moment. "I take it that Libby is his second wife," he said.

"That whore," Karen Bradbury hissed.

"Why come after me?" Fargo frowned.

"A bitch has no stud, she can't do much."

"It takes two to waltz," Fargo said. "Or did you figure to shoot her after you finished with me."

"No, but I thought about it. Shooting her would only hurt my pa. He loves her. He can't see her for what she is," the young woman said, bitterness coating her words.

"So you're going to keep her faithful by bullets. You're going to shoot anyone that lays her," Fargo said.

Karen Bradbury's finely molded lips tightened. "I hadn't thought that far but seeing you and her last night just made me crazy mad. You of all people, the man my pa hired."

"Explaining it doesn't excuse it, honey. You need a rein on that temper of yours," Fargo said.

Her eyes shot back light blue flame. "And you need one on something of yours," she shot back.

"Sassing is better than shooting but you're not giving any more of either," Fargo said, emptied the rifle, and handed it back to her. "Don't be coming after me again, honey."

"That means you're staying."

"Of course I'm staying. I was hired to come out here. Nothing's changed about that," Fargo said.

"Principles?" she slid at him tartly.

"What's wrong with that?"

"Just that you've a strange way of applying them," she sniffed.

"Maybe, but it's my way, honey," Fargo said.

Karen Bradbury studied him for a long moment. "You hold to your place. We might be friends under different circumstances," she said, her eyes softening. "But not with you screwing my pa's wife. I've principles, too."

"That might've been a one and only," Fargo said.

"You wouldn't promise that, would you?" she said, instant hopefulness in her eyes.

"Nope," he said.

"Go to hell," she flared and spun on her heel. His hand shot out, caught her by the elbow and pulled her back.

"Not so fast, Karen, honey. You can stay right there until I put some more clothes on or I can tie you up. Your choice," he said.

"Finish dressing," she said and he hurried on clothes.

"You've a horse somewhere," he said.

"Just down the hill."

"Let's go," he said and walked behind her, the

Ovaro following along. Her long, willow-wand body moved with easy grace, her tight, firm rear very much in keeping with the rest of her. She halted at a thicket and brought the horse out, and Fargo felt a moment of appreciation and surprise. No cow pony, the horse was a reddish bay thoroughbred, at least sixteen hands high, good breeding in his every movement and in the elegant arch of his neck. Karen Bradbury swung onto the horse with a smooth, fluid motion, her breasts hardly swinging. "Head for town," he said.

"Why?" she said and frowned.

"I'm thinking about taking you in," he said.

A moment of panic leaped into her light blue eyes. "You wouldn't. You can't," she protested.

"You tried to kill me," he said.

"I explained about that."

"And I told you, explaining doesn't count."

"Let me go, that's all you have to do," Karen said.

"Thanks," he said dryly and brought the Ovaro alongside her as they moved down the hillside. "Where'd you get that horse?" he asked.

"Bred him. He's from my stables," she said.

"You one of the horse farms I saw?"

"Yes. K-B Farm—hunters, jumpers, saddle horses. My mother left me enough money to get started. She knew it was something I always wanted to do," the young woman said.

They reached the road at the bottom of the hills, and he turned east toward Windsor Bell and saw the glower come into her handsome face. He rode in silence beside her when a horseman appeared from a cross-path and came toward them at a trot. The man rode a dark gray saddlebred, another good-looking animal of obviously good breeding. He drew to a halt and Fargo took in a young man, brown hair and long sideburns, a handsome enough face diluted by an air of arrogance that was emphasized by the slight sneer of his mouth. "Karen," he said. "Came visiting and you weren't there. Thought I'd look for you."

"Hello, Clay," Karen said and Fargo smiled inwardly at the glance of uncertainty she threw him. "This is Clay Sanborn," she introduced.

"Skye Fargo." The Trailsman nodded and saw Clay Sanborn's quick glance at Karen.

"Something wrong?" he asked her and Fargo smiled. Sanborn could be sharp enough to pick up something unsaid in the young woman's face. Or he knew Karen Bradbury very well. It was the first, Fargo decided.

"We had a disagreement," Karen told him. "He thinks some time in a jail cell would be good for me."

Clay Sanborn frowned with shocked indignation as he turned to Fargo. "That's ridiculous," he snapped. "Do you know who this young lady is?"

"I know who she is," Fargo said.

"Then how can you possibly think she needs time in jail? Or think that'll happen?" Sanborn returned.

"She tried to kill me," Fargo said. "That makes me very irritable."

Sanborn turned his frown on Karen.

"I thought he was someone else," she said with a quick glance at Fargo that held a glimmer of plea in it.

"Then it was all a mistake," Sanborn said and she nodded. "Forget it, Mister," he said to Fargo.

"Not ready to do that," Fargo said.

"The decision's been made. I'll see the young lady home," Sanborn said, the arrogance in his face moving into his tone.

"It's not your affair, cousin. Get lost," Fargo said.

"Of course it's my affair, as a friend of Karen's and as a gentleman," Sanborn said.

"Go be a gentleman someplace else," Fargo said.

"It's plain you're not one and you don't know how we treat a lady here."

"Maybe not but she stays with me," Fargo said.

"Now, look here—" Sanborn began but Fargo cut him off.

"Drop it, Sanborn," he said and smiled pleasantly. But Sanborn's face remained imperious. The sharpness he'd shown with Karen had vanished. He didn't pick up the ice behind the smile. He'd let arrogance dull acuity, Fargo saw. But Karen Bradbury could read signs also, and Fargo heard her voice interject itself.

"It's all right, Clay. I can take care of this myself," she said.

Clay Sanborn's eyes stayed on Fargo, disdain in his face. "I still think he needs to be taught some proper Kentucky manners," he muttered.

"I'll give you a chance to do that some other time," Fargo said.

"And I'll enjoy doing just that," the man said.

"Good. Now move," Fargo growled.

Sanborn turned to Karen. "You sure you don't want me to give this lout a thrashing right now?" he asked.

"Please, Clay. Just leave," she said with annoyance clear in her voice. Clay Sanborn turned his mount and rode off in a canter. Fargo watched him disappear around a bend and moved the Ovaro forward again.

"He owes you a debt," Fargo said and her silence was proof that she understood. "He special?" Fargo queried.

"He comes calling," Karen said.

"Can't blame him for that," Fargo said.

"Compliments?" she asked. "That's a surprise."

"Just observation," he said as he rode down the road. The buildings of Windsor Bell came into sight when they turned a long curve and he reined to a halt. "Get," he grunted.

"You letting me go?" She frowned. "You're not taking me in?"

"That's right," he said.

Her light blue eyes bored into him. "Why this change of heart?"

"Not for your sake," Fargo said. "But you're right. There'd have to be explaining. I figure there's no need to hurt a man without a good reason."

"Thank you," Karen Bradbury said very quietly.

"Hightail it before I change my mind," he growled. She turned and put the reddish bay into a trot. She rode damn well, he noted, one with her horse and no straining about her. When she rode from sight he moved the Ovaro on toward town. Windsor Bell was bustling when he rode in, wearing an even greater air of respectability by day than it did by night with almost as many surreys and light pony wagons as working rigs. He drew up before Sam Bradbury's house and Libby opened the door at his knock, a low-necked white blouse tight around her deep breasts.

"The mayor's come back. He's in the study," she said and paused in the hallway with him, her voice dropping to a whisper. "He's real tired. He'll sleep like a log tonight. I could meet you somewhere," she said.

"I don't know. He may have me doing something tonight. "I'll let you know later," Fargo said, and she pressed the deep, pillowy breasts into him for a moment and he felt their warm softness.

"God, last night has all my juices running. Find a time and place and soon," she said, stepped back, and led the way down the corridor. She showed him into a wood-paneled room with some bookshelves and an ornate wood desk. The man rose from behind the

41

desk, tall yet stooped, hair still mostly black, a narrow figure with a long face deeply lined. It was a face that had once held strength, he guessed, but now he saw only tiredness in it and eyes that wore pain and sadness even when they smiled.

"Sorry I was away when you arrived," Sam Bradbury said. "They caught a bank robber down in Red Sands and I went to question him about what's been happening here. I decided he wasn't part of anything up here."

"Just what is going on here? So far somebody had me drygulched, and they tried to beat me senseless in a saloon fight," Fargo said, and Sam Bradbury's eyes grew more tired as he sat down heavily in the chair. "Seems everybody knows you sent for me. You put up a public notice?" Fargo asked sharply.

"I'm real sorry for whatever happened. I had to inform a number of people and I guess the word just got out," the mayor said.

"It sure did. Maybe you ought to tell me why you sent for me. I don't see a town that needs a trailsman," Fargo said.

"But we do," Sam Bradbury said. "We've been hit with robbery after robbery. Anything valuable that gets shipped to the bank or from the bank gets hit, cash profits, payroll monies, gold, silver, you name it."

"That sounds like a job for a sheriff," Fargo said.

"It does and I'm both mayor and sheriff. But it only sounds that way. The varmints that hit us ride into the hills and disappear."

"Disappear?"

"That's right. Now I know no gang of cutthroats can disappear but it's also plain that we haven't been able to pick up their trail or their tracks. We need

42

somebody who can read trails other man can't see. That's why I sent for you."

"Who's we."

"Every rancher, cattleman, horse breeder, cotton mill owner, gold and copper miner this side of the valley. As mayor, they look to me to do something and everything I've tried has failed. That doesn't make anybody happy. My job could be on the line," Sam Bradbury said, and Fargo saw defeat and tiredness in his long face.

"Any leads at all?" he questioned.

"No leads but plenty of theories," the mayor said. "Now that you're here I'll call a meeting so you can meet with everybody. The offer I made you still stands, Fargo."

Fargo took only a moment to consider. The money was not the kind to turn down. Besides, there's been two attempts on his life. He had his own score to settle. "You've a deal," he said, and Sam Bradbury let out a sigh of relief.

"Everything will be on hold for the next three days. Nobody will be shipping anything while the fair is on. Maybe you should come to the fair, look around, keep your eyes open. As an outsider, you might see things we don't," the mayor said.

"Good enough. How about that meeting?"

"Here, the night after the fair ends," Bradbury said, and after a handshake, Fargo left the room to see Libby at the front door. He found himself with a strange conflict of emotions. He felt a little awkward about bedding the mayor's wife, now that he'd met the man. Sam Bradbury was plainly a hollow shell, basically a good man consumed with his own inadequacies and now afraid of losing his job. But he felt for Libby too. She was consumed with unsatisfied hungers. She needed help also. He hadn't turned down the mayor's plea for help. He didn't see how he could turn down Libby. That wouldn't be fair, he told himself. Rationalization was a wonderful thing, especially when it let you do what you wanted to do in the first place.

"Take the small road north at ten tonight. I'll meet you," he told her as he brushed by and walked from the house. He took the Ovaro through town and out the other end to Barnaby's shack where the old-timer was just feeding the gray mare.

"Cup of coffee?" Barnaby asked.

"I'd appreciate that," Fargo said and followed the thatch of white hair into the shack. The coffee was fresh and bracing and Fargo relaxed in an old and worn yet still comfortable stuffed chair. "Met the mayor," he said. "Got anything to add to what he told me?"

"No, except that he's in trouble if this thing isn't stopped. You're his last chance, I'd guess.

"What can you tell me about Karen Bradbury?" Fargo questioned.

"Smart, strong, knows what she wants and how to get it. Was that way as a youngster," Barnaby said.

"What about her and Libby?" Fargo asked. "There's no love lost between them. I know that much."

"That's putting it mildly. Karen feels that Libby's a gold-digging tramp who married Sam only because he was the mayor and could give her security and community standing."

"What do you think?"

"I think that's pretty much so," Barnaby said.

"Karen move out after Bradbury married Libby?" Fargo asked.

"No, she already had her own horse farm then. But that didn't stop her from hating Libby. Karen was always the one to protect her pa and she became more so after her ma died."

"Then Libby took over the role," Fargo said.

"But not to Karen. She feels she's still the only one who really cares about her pa."

"She might be right there," Fargo thought aloud. "Did you know her mother?"

"I did. Fine woman. A real lady," Barnaby said. He reached over and turned a small lamp on as the night began to drop over the land. Fargo rose as he finished the coffee.

"Thanks for filling me in," he said.

"Anytime," Barnaby said, and Fargo left with the feeling that the old man harbored a lot of still unsaid wisdom about the town and its environs. The night stayed warm as he rode into the low hills and found a secluded spot between two red mulberry where he warmed some beef jerky over a small fire. He ate leisurely and when he finished he left his bedroll stretched out on the ground and rode down to the narrow road north of town.

He didn't have to wait long before he saw the lone horse and rider moving toward him under a pale moon. He moved from the side of the road and Libby saw him and turned to him at once. She wore a long duster that completely covered her and she followed him to the trees in silence. He dismounted, watched her swing from her horse, and step to the bedroll where she whisked off the long duster to reveal a white silk nightgown beneath it, her deep breasts spilling over the low, lacy top. He was pulling off clothes as she slid the straps of the nightgown from her shoulders and the garment fell to her feet and she sank down onto the bedroll, her earthy, full-fleshed body radiating desire.

Libby was all the eager, thirsting wantonness she

had been the night before, her body shaking and pushing, low groans coming in deep spasms to match her
every thrusting, arching gratification, and finally her
last, groaning cry drifted into the night and she lay
panting beside him. She fell asleep with him, warm
and soft against him, and he woke and took her back
to the edge of town before night ended.

"Where and when, big man?" Libby asked before
she rode on.

"I don't know. I'll have to wait and see," Fargo
said.

"Don't be too long. I don't like waiting," she said
and he caught the touch of dictation in her voice.

"I'll remember that," he said and when he rode
back to the bedroll in the hills his lips were a thin
line. Little Libby had delusions she could equate passion with possession, getting a man in bed with getting
her way. But then she wasn't the first one to make
that error. She'd learn better.

3

It was mid-morning when he wandered down to the fairgrounds where poles and pennants had been erected. Food booths were being set up and he walked the Ovaro through the preparations. He had circled to the perimeter of the area when he saw Barnaby helping a woman roll two barrels to a wood booth. " 'Morning," Barnaby called out as Fargo came closer. "Just giving Aggie a hand," the man said as he straightened up. "Everything starts tomorrow."

"So I see." Fargo nodded. "Looks very festive."

"Don't tell me you plan to enter some of the events," the voice cut in and Fargo turned to see Clay Sanborn, Karen Bradbury standing alongside him. She wore a light blue shirt that matched her eyes as it clung to her willowy figure and outlined the long curve of her breasts.

"Hadn't planned on it," Fargo said.

A half-sneer twisted Clay Sanborn's mouth. "Karen tells me you're the one the mayor hired. Can't say I think much of his choice but it was left in his hands," the man said. Fargo turned a glance to the young woman. She met his eyes with calm coolness.

"You know I want you out of here," she said.

"You give any reasons?" Fargo smiled.

Karen Bradbury's eyes narrowed a fraction but her reply was cloaked in cool composure. "I don't get the feeling you're terribly trustworthy," she said.

"Too bad but it's what your pa thinks that counts," Fargo said.

"Perhaps he's not as good a judge of character as I am," she said almost offhandedly.

"And maybe you're not as good a judge as you think?" he countered.

"Look here, old boy," Clay Sanborn's voice interrupted. "Let's make it a sporting proposition. There are three major events at the fair. Enter one of them. Win and I'll see you get an added bonus. Lose and you do what the young lady wants . . . ride out of here."

Fargo shot a glance at Barnaby and saw the warning in the man's eyes. "What are the three events?" he asked.

"First, the race. Three miles of hard riding and jumping," Sanborn said.

Fargo ran one hand down the jet black neck of the Ovaro. "This horse knows jumping," he said. Clay Sanborn's smile was a mixture of disdain and anticipation and Fargo heard Barnaby cut in.

"You'd be riding against the finest jumpers in the state," the old-timer said.

"That's true. You'd be riding against me," Sanborn said.

"And me," Karen put in. "I won the last two hurdle races."

Fargo smiled and thought for a moment. He knew the quality of the horses they'd bring—fast, well-bred, and well-schooled but used to gentleman's jumping where the climate was proper and mannered. "What are the other two events?" he asked.

"A sharpshooting contest, rifle and pistol," Sanborn said.

"He's won it for the last four years," Barnaby said.

"We don't need your comments," Sanborn said sharply.

"Fair's fair," Barnaby snapped back.

"The last event?" Fargo queried.

"Fighting Mountain Man Joe, a bare-handed match," Sanborn said.

Barnaby cut in again. "He's big, mean, and strong. Nobody's ever beaten him."

Sanborn voice took on a sneer. "I think they're all too rich for Fargo's blood. But I expected as much."

Fargo's eyes went to Karen and saw the tiny furrow on her brow as she studied him. He smiled inwardly. "You've anything to say?" he asked.

"You could get lucky," she said.

He let his smile show. She didn't share Clay Sanborn's confident arrogance. She was a lot more astute than he was. But she didn't want to miss a chance to get him away from Libby. His eyes stayed on her a moment longer. There was a smoldering, banked fire under her outer coolness, as surely as there were lovely breasts under her tailored shirt. He returned his eyes to Clay Sanborn. "How about a little side bet?" he said.

The man's brows lifted. "A separate wager in addition? I've no objections. "What'd you have in mind?"

"You said let's make it a sporting proposition. I'll enter all three events. I win them all I get the pleasure of the little lady in bed," Fargo said.

Sanborn's face darkened in anger. "Good God, man, betting a lady's honor. No gentleman would make such a wager."

"You already told me I was no gentleman," Fargo said. "That's the deal. Take it or leave it."

"I won't have anything to do with it," Sanborn said. "You ought to be horsewhipped for suggesting it."

"Then I'll just stay on and do what I was hired to do," Fargo shrugged.

"Wait a minute," Karen cut in. "You lose any of the three events you ride out and don't come back."

"That's right," Fargo said evenly.

"It's a deal," Karen said, defiance in the light blue eyes.

"Karen!" Sanborn exploded. "You can't be a party to a wager such as that."

"Simmer down, Clay," she said and her eyes stayed on the big man in front of her. "I don't think he'll win one event, but he certainly isn't going to win all three. I'm not the slightest bit concerned."

"That's nice," Fargo said blandly and saw her eyes narrow. "Now I'd like to go over the course," he said.

She pointed to a wide opening in the trees at the far end of the fair site. "It starts there and circles back. The finish line is right where we're standing," Karen said.

"Much obliged," he said and nodded and let the Ovaro move forward. Barnaby fell in beside him and he glanced back to where Karen and Sanborn faced each other.

"Sometimes I don't understand you at all, Karen," he heard Sanborn say. "That just wasn't a wager for a proper young lady to make."

"Oh, be quiet, Clay. I just tripled our chances to get rid of him. That's proper enough for me," Karen snapped back and rode off. Fargo smiled as he and Barnaby reached the start of the course and he was aware of Barnaby's disapproving stare.

"Think I made a mistake?" he asked.

"I couldn't believe what I heard. You've got to be the biggest damfool this side of Oregon or the best man I've ever seen," Barnaby said.

"Maybe some of both." Fargo laughed and put the

horse into a trot as Barnaby continued to shake his head. He slowed when he reached the first hurdle, a post-and-rail fence of more than average height. He circled around it, carefully sizing up every inch of it and went on. The next jump was an open ditch with a high hurdle of haystacks in front of it, a tricky jump that could take many a horse down. Once again, he examined it carefully, imprinting distances in his mind, and went on to the next hurdle, a stone wall. Two lower fence jumps were next and then a double-oxer, the first pole almost four feet, high brush behind it and the second pole a few inches over four feet.

It would be one of the hardest, he grunted as he went on to find a triple bar came next with a five-foot spread. A stone-and-brush jump was next and, as the course curved back to the fairgrounds, a stone-and-log jump appeared. An open space followed for the speed horses to gather themselves and then a brush-and-water jump with at least a six-foot spread. Farther on he came to a hogback of three poles, the highest center pole at four feet, the spread a little over five feet. Natural rail fences completed the last of the three jumps before the finish line came into view. "Good hard course," he said to Barnaby as they reached the end of the track.

"Sorry you opened your mouth?" Barnaby asked.

"No," Fargo said. "I'm counting on human nature as much as horseflesh." He didn't amplify the remark and Barnaby accepted it with a wry smile.

"There were others standing by. You can bet that the news is all over town now and it'll be all over the county by tomorrow. There'll be a bigger than usual crowd to see this race," Barnaby said.

"Fine with me," Fargo said.

"You're welcome to bunk in with me and get a night's rest under a roof," Barnaby offered.

"Thanks. I might just do that," Fargo said. "If I don't, I'll see you here come morning. I forgot to ask what time it starts."

"Riders can enter anytime up to ten o'clock. Race time is ten-thirty," Barnaby said and Fargo rode on with a wave. He rode into the first row of low hills, found a stream, and dismounted. Using the gear from his saddlebag, he washed, brushed and curried the Ovaro, finishing with the hoof pick and the stable rubber. He had worked leisurely and the day was drawing to a close when he rode the gleaming, glistening horse into town. He had come to the mayor's house when the door opened and Sam Bradbury rushed out, his long face deepened with worry lines. Libby came close behind him.

"Dammit, Fargo, I heard about that damn wager you made with my daughter," the man shouted. "What the hell ever got into you? I hired you to do a job not make damn fool wagers."

"You worried about your daughter paying or my losing?" Fargo asked.

"I'm worried about your losing. Karen can do anything she wants," the man said.

"I don't aim to lose," Fargo said.

"Dammit, you better not," Sam Bradbury said and stormed back into the house. Libby stayed, her eyes surveying Fargo with faint amusement.

"I'll make the same bet with you she did," Libby said.

"I don't need that for you, honey," he said.

"Bastard," Libby bit out, her face darkening in anger. "Don't bother coming around again," she called after him as he rode on.

"Whatever you say," he tossed back as the darkness closed around him. He decided to forgo Barnaby's offer for this night and he stopped in at the saloon to get something to eat and found the place buzzing with wagers. A moment of silence greeted him as he sat down but the betting began quickly enough again. He listened with wry amusement as he ate. Most of the bettors were picking him to lose but one slightly built, sandy-haired man kept taking wagers he'd win each event. When the betting finally tapered off and he'd finished his meal, he drifted to where the man was arranging his betting slips. "Thanks for the confidence," Fargo said. "I'm wondering why."

"Jack Sanders," the man introduced himself. "First, I like betting on long shots. Second, you don't seem a man who'd take on something he didn't feel he could do. Third, I've seen that Ovaro of yours. I've a feeling he can out-hustle those fancy jumpers."

"That takes care of the race. What about the shooting contest?"

"A range hand I know said he saw you in a shoot-out down Texas way once, said you were real good," Sanders answered.

"Well, you've got some reasons behind your stand." Fargo smiled. "That leaves the fight."

Jack Sanders wrinkled his face. "That's the one I'm most worried about," he said.

"Barnaby Olsen says Mountain Man Joe is big, strong, and mean," Fargo said.

"He's all those things."

"Anything else you can tell me about him?" Fargo pressed and the man creased his brow in thought.

"He's dumb, real dumb. Maybe that's why he's so hard to beat. No sense, no feeling," Sanders said.

Fargo let his thoughts turn for a moment. Perhaps Sanders have given him something more important than he realized. "Much obliged," he said rising, and Sanders shook his hand.

"Good luck, for both of us," the man said and

Fargo made his way from the saloon. He rode slowly, into the first tier of low hills, found the place between the sycamores, and laid out his bedroll. After unsaddling the Ovaro he shed clothes and slept quickly. He wanted all the rest he could get. It would be a race that'd take a lot out of both horse and rider, he knew. He slept heavily, letting the body draw deep of its own strengths until he woke with the morning sun.

He breakfasted lightly on two apples, golden yellow Grimes with their juicy, slightly tart flavor and slowly made his way down to the fairgrounds. His thoughts turned to the past, several years back, when he had run a similar race. But he had only one real threat to worry about then. This time there'd be two, at least, Sanborn and Karen. He suspected they might work together to try and defeat him and he hoped they would. With their attention on him, instead of concentrating on running their own races, they'd be vulnerable. He already had his own plans made and he felt the excitement catch at the magnificent Ovaro as the horse sensed the impending race. Forelegs prancing, he stepped his way through the gathering crowd to the registration table where Fargo leaned from the saddle to sign in. When he finished he saw Karen nearby, her eyes on him, astride a fine-looking bay. His eyes moved over the horse. Plenty of speed in the animal's conformation, he noted, but not a great deal of power. He had the lines of a jumper but he'd tire near the finish, Fargo concluded.

Clay Sanborn rode up on a tan mount with the same good speed lines as Karen's horse but with more substance, shoulders carrying more muscle. They'd both be tough horses to beat but he half-smiled as he saw Sanborn and Karen keep distance between them as they talked, confirmation of what he'd expected. Both their mounts were high-strung, skittish solo performers, neither accustomed to nor liking close contact, the strength of a range horse. He let his gaze travel across the other horses beginning to line up. They were all thoroughbreds, all with the balance of qualities that made for good jumpers. They were all a threat. He wouldn't discount any of them.

His eyes scanned the riders. They were a different picture, most of them young, some stable boys, some farmhands, all no doubt chosen because they were light and good with their horses. He saw one other young woman, small of build and wearing a black velvet riding cap. But none had time to gather much experience, he was certain. He counted sixteen in all as he walked the pinto to the starting line. Karen came alongside him on his right and Clay Sanborn on his left two horses away. Karen allowed a cool nod as he grinned at her. "You could come in second," he said. "That's not too bad." Light blue fire flashed in her eyes before she looked away. The starter had come onto the track and the crowd pressed forward on both sides. He saw three men atop trees with bullhorns. They were going to keep the onlookers informed of the race as the horses left their sight.

The starter raised his hand, the pistol in it. Fargo put his forearm against the Ovaro's withers and felt the slight tremble. The horse was eager to go. The pistol exploded with a sharp crack and the line of horses charged forward. Fargo saw Clay Sanborn's tan mount take the lead at once, Karen edging out in front of him. He applied a gentle touch to the Ovaro's reins to hold him in. "Easy, boy, no need to use up too much energy now," he murmured and he felt the horse respond by slacking off a fraction. Sanborn stayed in the lead but three other horses followed on his heels and Fargo let them edge in front of him.

Karen, still off to the side, was also holding her bay back a little, he saw.

Three of the other horses passed Sanborn and two more came up fast. The first obstacle came into sight, the post-and-rail fence and he smiled as he saw the three lead horses slow before attacking the jump. They took the fence cleanly but slowing cost them at least ten seconds and Sanborn was abreast of them as he landed on the other side of the jump. He saw Karen take the fence with ease and he let the Ovaro sail over it with plenty of room to spare. He cast a glance behind to see everyone had cleared the fence. He kept a steady pace a little behind Karen and to her left and the next jump appeared, the haystacks and the open ditch behind them. The stacks completely obscured the ditch and he watched the first three horses jump. One made it cleanly, the other two went down as they hit the ditch on the other side. Sanborn and Karen took it without trouble and the Ovaro had to stretch only a little to hurdle the spread.

He heard the sound and shouts behind him as two more horses went down. The lead horse slowed again as it neared the stone wall and again lost precious seconds as Clay Sanborn sailed his mount over the stones. Fargo's eyes went to Karen and he nodded in silent appreciation as her horse took the wall with ease. He jumped cleanly and stayed behind her as the field raced for the next two natural-fence jumps. Everyone took them both without trouble and Fargo saw the young boy aboard the lead horse began to gather himself for the double-oxer that rose up ahead. He was cautious and once again slowed to give his mount time to gather itself. Clay Sanborn leaped past him and Karen came abreast of him as he jumped. Both Sanborn and Karen spurted into the lead when they hit the ground on the other side of the jump.

Fargo took the hurdle with plenty of room to spare and he was even with the young boy when he landed on the other side.

Fargo saw the boy throw a glance at him and touch a riding crop to his horse's rump. The animal surged forward as Fargo held his place. Sanborn and Karen were a dozen feet ahead as they reached the triple bar and he saw both clear the jump. But this time the boy didn't slow his mount and Fargo grimaced, certain what would happen. His eyes were on the horse as the animal jumped, slammed into the center bar, and went down. This was a horse used to slowing a fraction to gather itself before jumping. The boy had made the mistake of not allowing that. He leaped past the horse and rider on the ground and the pinto landed lightly and was instantly in full stride. Fargo heard another horse go down at the triple bar behind him.

Sanborn and Karen glanced back at him as he let the Ovaro open up a little and gain some distance on them. They didn't panic and kept their mounts going smoothly. The stone-and-log jump came into sight. It was higher than it appeared he remembered, and he admired the ease with which Sanborn and Karen took the obstacle. A faint pressure of his knees against the Ovaro just before the start of the jump warned the horse to stretch and he cleared the jump with room to spare. The next half-mile was unobstructed racing room, but he kept the Ovaro some dozen feet behind Karen's bay and Sanborn's tan mount. Both threw glances back at him and he saw Karen's frown. He wasn't doing what they expected, using up his horse's strength in an effort to pass them, which is what they wanted. They rode speed mounts that could stay in front, perhaps draw away.

But he stayed back, dogged their heels, and they

didn't open up distance as the brush-and-water jump appeared. This was probably the trickiest jump of all, the spread six feet and real hard for rider and horse to measure. Karen and Sanborn leaned forward as they concentrated on the jump and took it almost in unison. But he saw the left hindfoot of Sanborn's horse touch the brush and drag through it. The horse was tiring and just about the time Fargo expected it would. Fargo half-rose in the stirrups as the Ovaro approached the jump, let the horse go full-out, and the Ovaro rose and flew over the jump with both height and length to spare. He glanced back when he landed and saw three horses go down and one balk and throw its rider.

The hogback was next and Sanborn's horse had dropped a few paces behind Karen. The animal was clearly tired but it was a good enough jumper to take the hogback, Fargo was certain. Karen's bay was first over, a clean jump, and Sanborn followed, his mount's hind feet brushing the center pole. Fargo measured the jump, the center log the highest, the kind of jump that could deceive a horse. But the Ovaro's power carried him over and as he landed, Fargo saw Karen glance back at him. He flicked a hand against the horse's rump and the Ovaro charged forward, closing distance as the first of the three last rail fences loomed up. He smiled as he saw Karen and Clay Sanborn exchange quick glances. They began to move their mounts closer together and took the first fence almost side by side. Fargo took the jump right on their heels and sent the Ovaro forward close behind them as the second fence came up fast.

With a surge, he sent the Ovaro charging forward through the narrow space between Karen's and Sanborn's mounts. He felt his right leg brush against Karen as the Ovaro came up against both horses, tight quarters shoulder-to-shoulder contact. Both horses reacted exactly as Fargo expected they would. Sanborn's mount yanked his head around so violently it almost took the reins from his rider's hands as he bolted to the left. Fargo heard Karen's cry of surprise and anger as her horse swerved to the right. Fargo took the fence full-out as Karen and Sanborn struggled to get their horses back in position to jump. Looking back, he saw that they barely managed to do so, Sanborn's horse almost falling as he took the jump. Their maneuver to keep him behind them hadn't merely failed. It had backfired. But he saw Karen call on the last burst of speed from her horse and the animal closed distance fast as the last fence rose up a dozen yards away.

Her horse was blowing hard but it was a real speed horse and she was almost abreast of him. Fargo touched the pinto gently with his knee and the horse veered right. He heard Karen fling a curse into the air as her mount shied away at once, tried to turn before she managed to bring it back under control. She had lost at least ten seconds and was still on the other side of the last fence as Fargo cleared it and saw the finish line in the distance. He shot a glance back to see Karen had cleared the fence, Sanborn now a poor third, and he saw her use her riding crop on her horse. The mount reacted and Fargo saw there was still speed in the animal. He turned back to hunch down low in the saddle, loosen the reins, and let the Ovaro go all out, powerful hindquarters driving it forward in a last burst of power and speed. He heard Karen's horse coming up behind him but the animal was panting heavily, unable to gain any more distance.

The cheers of the crowd filled the air as Fargo swept across the finish line and slowly pulled the Ovaro to a canter. He glanced back to see Karen cross, her horse slowed and heaving and he reined the pinto to a trot, then a walk, and made a circle. He halted, let the horse draw in deep drafts of air, and then walked the lathered animal in a slow circle so he wouldn't cramp up. The crowd was still cheering and his eyes swept the faces in the front row and saw Jack Sanders. The man raised his arm into the air as he grinned happily.

Karen had dismounted and walked her horse toward him, her eyes narrowed but he saw the grudging admiration in their light blue orbs. "Good ride," she said.

"The best laid plans of mice and men . . ." he said blandly.

"I don't know what you mean," she said coolly.

"Whatever you say, honey." Fargo smiled and she turned away, her lips tightening against each other. He walked on, passed Sanborn who sullenly avoided his glance. Barnaby pushed through the crowd to him.

"My hat's off to you, Fargo," he said. "You outrode them and outsmarted them."

"And I've a tired horse that needs a day's rest. I'm kind of tuckered out myself," Fargo said. "But I might take you up on that room and board tonight."

"I'll be expecting you," Barnaby said and Fargo walked on to see Sam Bradbury with Libby come toward him. The mayor's lined face was still troubled.

"That's one win, a big one, I'll admit. I'm still not happy about any of this, Fargo," he said.

"Keep the faith," Fargo said and his eyes went to Libby. She wore haughtiness around her. It didn't fit well; he smiled. "You, too, ma'm," he said and walked on and felt her glare follow. He rode slowly into the low hills where he had spotted a small, irregular-shaped lake. He unsaddled the horse and shed his own trousers and boots before leading the horse into the lake. The water was sun warmed yet refreshingly cool less than a foot below the surface. He let the horse stay in the lake for almost two hours, sometimes going out far enough so that the water came up to cover shoulder and stifle. Finally satisfied that the soothing, healing powers of the water had done its work on strained muscles and tendons he brought the Ovaro back onto the shore where the sun could work its own brand of restorative magic.

He stretched out and dozed until the sun slid down behind the high hills. He dressed and rode slowly down to Barnaby's place as night fell and the old man opened the door when he arrived. Fargo smelled the delicious odor of good cooking waft from the open door. "Thought you might need a meal," Barnaby said. "Rabbit cooked with bacon, nutmeg, onion, white wine, and mustard sauce."

"Where'd you learn to be a fancy chef?" Fargo said, stepping into the shack.

"Believe it or not, I was chef at the Hotel Dennis in St. Louis for three years," Barnaby said. "I've always liked to cook."

"Anything you haven't done," Fargo said as he sat down at a small wooden table set for two.

"Never won a race like you did today," Barnaby said. "I understand now what you meant about counting on human nature as much as horseflesh."

"It'll be different tomorrow. Pure skill, nothing more," Fargo said. "Fill me in on it."

"The rifle shoot is pretty much plain marksmanship. The pistol shoot combines accuracy and a time factor," Barnaby said. "Sanborn's had such a lock on it that there usually aren't more than three or four other contestants."

"Stationary targets, I take it," Fargo said.

"Not in the rifle shoot. They've rigged up a device that operates like a giant pendulum, the target on top of it that goes back and forth. When there's a standoff they increase the speed," Barnaby said.

"I like that. I'm a lot more used to shooting at moving targets than still ones," Fargo said as he pushed his plate back. "Mighty tasty," he added. "I'll be turning in now for a good sleep."

"That'll help make a steady eye and a steady hand." Barnaby nodded and showed Fargo to a small back room with a cot and a lamp, a curtain separating it from the rest of the shack. Fargo shed clothes and slept quickly, the little shack a securely comforting place. He didn't wake till he heard Barnaby rattling coffee mugs in the morning light. After breakfast, he took the big Sharps from its saddle holster, oiled and examined it and, satisfied, returned it to its scabbard. He did the same with the Colt .44 and finally rode to the fairgrounds with Barnaby beside him. Sanborn was already there, Karen standing apart, and Fargo tossed her a wide smile as he dismounted. Three men were nearby, each holding a rifle, two young ranch hands, he noted, and one a stocky, burly man who carried a big buffalo gun.

Fargo's gaze went to the target set in a cleared area, a circular plate at the end of a tall pole operated from behind a half dozen bales of hay. The plate was wood, he saw, with a metal circle in the center that obviously rang with every bullseye. A man approached with a sheet of paper and a pencil and Fargo signed in. "You're last to sign in so you'll be last to shoot," the man said and Fargo nodded. He took the rifle from its holster and walked to the shooting line chalked across the ground. One of the two young hands stepped forward and the pendulum target began to move.

"You get three shots to hit the center," Barnaby murmured to Fargo. The young boy fired, hit the wood of the round plate with his first shot, clanged the second into the center. He stepped back and the other youth fired and hit the center with his first shot. The burly man took two shots before he hit the center and it was Sanborn's turn. He fired almost casually and hit the bullseye with his first shot. Fargo positioned himself, hardly seemed to aim and the plate clanged at once as he fired. He stepped back and saw the round plate move back and forth considerably faster as the speed of the pendulum device was quickened. The first youth shot again, missed entirely with his first shot and hit the wood of the circular target with his next two. The second youth managed to nick the plate with his last shot for a weak clang but Fargo saw the judge nod. The burly man with his cumbersome buffalo gun missed all his three shots and Sanborn stepped up.

He aimed, followed the moving target, and fired and the center plate clanged. He stepped back with a faintly smug smile on his handsome face. Fargo took his place, brought the Sharps up, and fired almost without aiming but the plate clanged. He stepped back, saw Sanborn's face lose its smugness, and Fargo nodded pleasantly to Karen. She looked straight ahead, her face set tightly. The pendulum speed was increased again, this time almost twice as fast as it had been for the first round. The young boy missed his three shots and Sanborn stepped up. He swung from his waist as he followed the target with his rifle, fired and missed, paused, zeroed in again and missed again. Fargo watched as Sanborn gathered himself, took a moment more to aim and put his last shot into the center plate.

Fargo raised the big Sharps and grimaced. The damn target was a lot faster moving through the rifle sights. He waited, followed its path and heard the satisfying clang of metal. The onlookers had raised a loud murmur and he cast a glance at Clay Sanborn. The man tried to cloak nervousness with disdain and Fargo smiled broadly as his eyes returned to the pendulum. It was snapping the target plate back and forth with real speed now. "They can't make it go any faster than that," he heard Barnaby mutter.

Sanborn raised his gun, fired and missed, fired again and missed and cursed. But he tightened his aim, waited and swung the rifle sharply and his last shot rang the metal plate. There was no disdain in his face as he stepped back and drew a deep breath of relief. Fargo raised the Sharps, followed the back and forth swing of the target, and fired. His shot hit the plate and he lowered the rifle. "You're tied," Barnaby said and drew a frown from Fargo. "It doesn't matter whether you hit the target with your first or your last shot," Barnaby explained. Fargo shrugged and put the rifle back into the saddle holster. "The pistol shoot will decide it," Barnaby said and Fargo turned a glance at Karen. Her eyes wore a veil as she met his smile and he brought his gaze back to the field where a row of six whiskey bottles had been placed on the edge of a fence rail, each some six inches from the other.

The man who'd signed him in stepped forward. "Time counts in this event as well as marksmanship. You'll each have six shots. Each bottle counts for ten points. But each second you take is a point off. That means if you hit five bottles you have fifty points. If you take ten seconds doing it you finish with forty points. If you shoot carefully and hit all six bottles you'd have yourself sixty points. But if you take twenty seconds to aim and shoot you'd end with forty points too. So it comes down to how well you can combine speed and marksmanship. You all understand?"

"Perfectly," Sanborn said and Fargo nodded, his

eyes on the distant row of bottles. Sanborn would be precise, he guessed. He wasn't used to fast shooting and Fargo let a grim smile edge his lips as he brought his eyes back to Sanborn and saw the man draw a Remington-Beals Navy revolver from his holster. A six-shot, single-action gun with a brass trigger guard, it was no gun for fast drawing, its balance poor. But it was accurate and made a good gun for target shooting. He stepped back as Sanborn raised the pistol, took aim, paused for a moment longer and fired. The first bottle shattered and Sanborn aimed his next shot and hit the second bottle. He continued his careful shooting until he hit the fifth bottle and then Fargo saw him hasten his aim time, shoot too quickly, and miss the sixth bottle.

"Fifty target points," the Judge announced. "Eleven seconds time. Final score, thirty-nine points."

Fargo frowned at the rail. The bottom quarter of each of the first five bottles was still in place and he heard the judge speak to him. "Give us a minute to set up new bottles."

"Don't bother," Fargo said and saw the man's eyebrows go upward. Fargo drew the big Colt, stepped up to the firing line, peered at the rail, and the bottles become six gunslingers waiting to draw. He raised the revolver and began to fire, blasting off the six shots with but a split second between each. The bottom part left of each bottle shattered as one bullet after another smashed into it, the remaining whole bottle exploding into smithereens with his last shot. Fargo stepped back and dropped the Colt into its holster.

"Jesus," he heard the judge say, awe filling the man's voice. "That's sixty target points, seven seconds shooting time. Final score, fifty-three points. You win, Mister."

Fargo's glance caught Sanborn, the man's face stiff,

his jaw muscle throbbing. Fargo took a long step that brought him in front of Karen. "Getting worried, honey?" He grinned.

She refused to let emotion show in her lovely face but her eyes were thoughtful as she stared back at him. "Surprised," she allowed, turned on her heel and strode away, her willowy body held very straight.

"A hell of a show," the voice said at his elbow and he turned to see Barnaby. "You spending tonight at my place?" the old-timer asked.

"I'd like to," Fargo said. "Meanwhile, I'm going to enjoy the fair, all this good food, might even do some dancing."

"I'll see you at the shack tonight," Barnaby said and walked away. Fargo saw Libby, clothed in a low-necked white blouse and loose tan skirt, her eyes boring into him.

"Where's the mayor?" he asked.

"At home doing paperwork. He sent me to report back," Libby said and fell into step beside him.

"Do that. It'll make him happy," Fargo said.

"She's not worth the winning, you know. You need a real woman," Libby remarked.

"Didn't you tell me not to come around anymore?" he said.

"I tried with Sam last night again. You can't get water from a dry well," she said, bitterness in her voice. "I need you and you'll need me. She's not for you. Just wait and see."

She turned and walked quickly away, full hips swinging. Jealousy was a two-way street, he grunted. Only it wasn't that simple. Libby had real hungers and felt threatened by Karen. That made for hate. Karen was fueled by a possessive loyalty and the conviction that Libby was no good. That made for hate. Jealousy was only a by-product. He shook away thoughts of both women and devoted himself to enjoying the fair. He ate wonderful apple pie, drank good cider, and danced some in a square-dance session that seemed never to end, and finally, when the day began to wind down, he rode back to Barnaby's shack.

There was enough of last night's satisfying meal left to take care of what was left of his appetite and he and Barnaby had just finished eating when the clatter of hoofbeats drew to a halt outside. Fargo rose and stepped out of the shack with Barnaby to see Clay Sanborn on a good-looking gray gelding. He was making an effort to keep his usual disdain from his face, Fargo saw as he watched the man smile broadly and offer a pleasant nod. The effort was only partially successful as Sanborn handed a bottle to him. "Fine French brandy," Clay Sanborn said. "That was wonderful shooting today and damn fine riding yesterday. I thought I'd show you the meaning of Kentucky sportsmanship, Fargo."

"Can't object to that," Fargo said as he took the bottle.

"Of course, I'm not going to wish you luck tomorrow. I'm not that good a sportsman." Sanborn laughed.

"Wouldn't expect that," Fargo agreed.

"Karen told me to tell you to have an extra drink for her."

"Thanks," Fargo said and, with another friendly nod, Sanborn turned the horse and rode away.

"Surprised, I'll wager," Barnaby said as Fargo returned to the shack with him.

"Yes," Fargo admitted. "You're not, I take it."

"No. His kind set great store in good manners, sportsmanship, proper behavior."

"Nothing wrong in that," Fargo said.

"Only it's all surface shit. They think nothing of

cheating a man out of his home and land but they do it with good manners."

"You sound bitter, Barnaby."

"Only for friends of mine," the old-timer said as he uncorked the bottle and brought out two shot glasses. "But fine brandy is fine brandy and I'm going to enjoy it."

"I'll save mine until tomorrow's finished," Fargo said.

"Suit yourself, friend," Barnaby said as he downed a shot and let out a groan of pleasure.

"I'll be turning in," Fargo said as Barnaby filled his glass again.

"This is too good to stop at only one drink," Barnaby said. "See you in the morning."

Fargo left him, drew the curtain, and undressed quickly in the dark. He slept quickly, but not before he wondered how good a sportswoman Karen would be if he won tomorrow.

the living a moment on the table and ladder as it ... ... It was good enough.

"Just something?" Barnaby saw it, too, his face ... with a flash of recognition and almost forgotten pride.

4

The morning sun woke him and Fargo sat up and sniffed the air. There was no aroma of morning coffee and the shack was silent. He pulled on trousers and boots and went into the other room to see Barnaby hard asleep in his big chair, his breathing steady enough. "Time to get moving, old-timer," Fargo said and shook Barnaby by the shoulder. He shook him again before the older man's eyes came open and stared at him. Barnaby blinked at him, blinked again.

"Christ, I see two of you," Barnaby muttered as he sat up straighter and rubbed his eyes. He looked at Fargo again. "Only one of you now but you keep on moving around."

"How much brandy did you put away last night?" Fargo questioned.

"Four shot glasses," Barnaby said. "Hell, that's nothin' for me." He pushed himself to his feet, took a step forward and almost fell but managed to straighten out as Fargo took hold of his elbow. "Damn," Barnaby muttered, shook off Fargo's hand and walked across the cabin. He stumbled twice, swayed, and turned to face Fargo as he flexed his arms.

"Am I still moving?" Fargo asked.

"No," Barnaby said. "But you're a mite fuzzy and my arms feel like they're made of rubber." He came forward, managed not to stumble but his body moved heavily, as a man in a stupor. "Jesus, I've never felt like this, not even after a keg of whiskey."

"Try to hit me," Fargo said and Barnaby came at him, swung a left and a right and another left and Fargo saw the slowness of each punch. Barnaby halted and peered at him from under the white eyebrows. "What do you feel now?" Fargo asked.

"I can't get my arms to work right. I feel heavy and slow," Barnaby said, slumped heavily into his chair. "I don't think I can make it to see the fight, Fargo. Christ, I don't figure this at all."

"I think I do," Fargo said and picked up the bottle of brandy and peered at it. Barnaby hadn't lied. There wasn't much taken from the bottle. "So much for Kentucky sportsmanship," Fargo bit out, picked up the bottle of brandy, and held it for Barnaby to see.

"The damn stuff's been fixed?" Barnaby frowned and pushed to his feet.

"Only it was meant for me," Fargo said. "You can see now, right? Only you can't get yourself coordinated."

"That's about it," Barnaby said. Fargo swore silently. The effects would have been subtler in him because of his being fifty years younger. But they would have done what they were intended to do—destroy his normal coordination and generally slow his reflexes. The gift had been Clay Sanborn's insurance policy and Fargo's eyes grew cold as a midwinter lake as he wondered if Karen had been a part of it.

"Can you ride?" he asked Barnaby.

"It'd take a real effort," Barnaby said. "I feel that if I sleep for another few hours it'll wear off."

"It probably will. You do that," Fargo said. "I have to get moving."

"Come back, one way or the other," Barnaby said and Fargo nodded. He used the small well behind the shack to wash, ate some grapes Barnaby had in a bowl and rode the Ovaro slowly through the almost deserted town to the fairgrounds. He took in the crowd gathered around a large, cleared oval. It seemed as though half the county had turned out for this final event and Fargo moved the Ovaro forward as the nearest onlookers made a path for him. He halted at the edge of the oval and he saw Jack Sanders nearby. The man grinned at him and held his fist up.

"Good luck, Fargo. You've made me a pot full of money so far. Don't stop now," Sanders called. Fargo nodded and his eyes scanned the front row of onlookers, saw Libby, Sam Bradbury beside her, and closer to him, Clay Sanborn with Karen near him. Sanborn couldn't keep smugness from his face Fargo saw, but Karen's was a lovely mask. The mayor watched glumly, worry lines creasing his already lined face. Fargo swung from the saddle and let himself almost fall as he touched the ground. He saw the faint smirk cross Sanborn's face and felt the ice form inside him. But he walked into the oval slowly, feigning a moment of unsteadiness.

Mountain Man Joe stepped forward from the other side of the oval. He had been well named Fargo saw as he took in a huge figure, six feet four at least, he guessed. Mountain Man Joe had thick, long, unkempt black hair, a heavy-featured face with a flattened nose and small eyes that held a dull determination. He wore a white undershirt and black trousers and fat bulges protruded over his belt. Man Mountain Joe had too much fat on him but under the fat was hulking power, his arms thick as small trees, shoulders oxlike in size. But Jack Sanders had unwittingly told him how to fight this mountainous creature and Fargo had his strategy firmly in place. The real danger lay in avoiding the behemoth's blows.

Two men from the fair stepped forward as Fargo

71

faced Mountain Man Joe in the center of the oval. "We're not going to stand by and see anyone killed, but this is a no-holds-barred fight, gents. The winner is the one who's standing at the end," one of the men said. "Is that clear to you both?" Mountain Man grinned his answer and Fargo nodded and the two men stepped back. "Go to it," the one called out and the huge form charged, moving quickly for all his bulk. Fargo avoided the rush, snapped two left jabs into the heavy face, putting just enough into them to draw the man's anger. Mountain Man charged again, followed with a swooping left that Fargo parried, started to bring around his own left but had to duck away as the huge form barreled forward. He twisted, stuck one foot out and Mountain Man tripped over it to fall sprawling on his stomach.

Fargo stepped forward. It was a no-holds-barred contest he reminded himself, and his opponent would take every advantage of that. As Mountain Man pushed to his feet, Fargo sent a ripping left upward and the heavy face erupted in a red gash at one side. But the giant shape rose with a bellow of fury and the tree-trunk arms flailed at Fargo who gave ground, ducked, and twisted away, returned to light jabs and dove away again. Mountain Man paused, came forward, struck out with roundhouse rights and lefts that made Fargo give ground again. The heavy form continued to move forward, punching, swinging wild blows, trying uppercuts and Fargo parried or ducked all of them as he backpedaled.

He halted suddenly, dropped under a swinging right and shot out his own uppercut. It landed flush on Mountain Man's jaw, a blow that would have dropped most men. But the heavy face only shuddered and came forward and Fargo ducked away, but his foe kicked out and Fargo felt the pain of the blow against his calf. He slowed for a split second, but it was time enough for his opponent to crash sideways into him. Fargo felt himself knocked off-balance and as he tried to recover he slipped and landed on one knee. He had time only to glance around when the huge form crashed into him and he went sprawling. Mountain Man had one arm wrapped around his legs and he rolled and Fargo felt himself being flipped onto his back.

The man lifted a tree-trunk arm and brought a tremendous blow down into Fargo's chest, and Fargo felt as though a mule had kicked him. As the pain shot through him, Mountain Man pushed forward with his body and Fargo felt the weight drive his breath from him. The man jammed a huge forearm against Fargo's throat and Fargo tried to use his legs to push out from under him but found he couldn't budge. What little breath he had left was fast leaving him but his right arm was somehow still free. He brought it around, extended one knuckle of his fist, and rammed it into Mountain Man's eye.

With a bellow of pain, the behemoth jerked his body backward. It was for but a split second but Fargo felt the forearm against his throat draw back and the tremendous weight over him shift slightly. He drew up one leg, drove his knee into the man's belly, and the huge figure slid from him. Fargo twisted himself free, rolled, rolled again and came up on his feet as Mountain Man pushed himself up. He had to stick to his plan, Fargo realized. He couldn't take any more risks until the time was ripe. As Mountain Man charged again, Fargo avoided two massive roundhouse blows, slipped away from each, and feigned and drew another wild swing. He danced away, jabbed lightly, and danced away again as his breath slowly returned. But the middle of his breastbone still throbbed with the pain of that tremendous blow. Fargo backpedaled again as Mountain Man charged, continued to back and circle, back and circle, flicking out light jabs that had no effect on his huge foe.

He ducked, feinted, twisted away, danced backward and Mountain Man Joe swung roundhouse punch after punch, looping some, trying to hook others, each a tremendous, crushing blow if landed. But Fargo stayed out of reach and Mountain Man was lumbering forward now, his mouth open, his breath coming in rasping gasps. He tried charging and Fargo easily avoided each rush and saw the man was gulping in air. He was thoroughly winded but he continued his wild swings and bull-like rushes. It was the only way he knew to fight. Jack Sanders had said he was stupid. Fargo let him throw two more desperate hooks and dug his own heels into the ground, ducked and shot a sizzling blow upward that smashed into the heavy face. A stream of "claret" spurted from the man's mouth and Fargo ducked another swing, shot a hard straight left that opened a cut across the man's eyebrow.

Like a wounded buffalo at bay, Mountain Man shook his head and swayed as he tried to gulp in air. He had exhausted himself and his strength was only dead weight now. Fargo feinted to the left and his foe started to swing but his awkward blows were only ponderous attempts now. Fargo shot a right hook across that ripped open the man's cheekbone. He drove two more straight punches into the center of the heavy face and stepped back. Mountain Man Joe's little eyes tried to peer through the curtain of red that ran down his face. Fargo set himself, drove a tremendous left hook into the heavy jaw and for the first time, the mountainous form staggered backward. Fargo shifted his aim and sent a pile driver right into the fold of fat that hung over the man's belt. With a groaning gasp, Mountain Man dropped to both knees, swayed there for a moment and then pitched forward onto his face. He lay motionless, except for the heaving of his thick midsection and Fargo stepped to him, pushed his foot under the man's chest and pushed the huge form onto its back.

Mountain Man lay with his eyes closed, his stomach shuddering, the features of his face almost indistinguishable. Fargo drew a deep breath, aware of the stillness of the crowd as they looked on in awe and suddenly the stillness exploded in a roar of cheers. "You win, Mister," one of the men said and Fargo drew his own deep breath and felt the pain in his chest and suddenly his arms and shoulders hurt, excitement no longer masking pain. He turned, found Karen and looked for Clay Sanborn, but the man was nowhere to be seen. He walked to Karen and saw her watch him approach with her eyes narrowed.

"Where's Sanborn?" he asked coldly.

"I don't know. I was watching you and when I looked for him he was gone," Karen said.

"Get your horse and come with me," Fargo said.

Her eyes took on blue fire. "Look, you may have won, but I'll pay up when I'm ready," she said.

"You flatter yourself. This has nothing to do with that. Just come along," he said and she saw the tightness in his face. He left her and walked to the Ovaro, nodded at those who shouted congratulations at him and he winced as he pulled himself into the saddle. Karen appeared on the bay she had ridden during the race and fell into step alongside him as he rode back through Windsor Bell in grim silence. When he dismounted at Barnaby's shack she couldn't keep the curiosity in her face as he motioned her inside with him. Barnaby was still in the chair, but he was awake and the question was instant on his lips.

"Let's have it, boy," he said.

"I won," Fargo said and Barnaby let out a half-shout, half-chuckle. "How are you feeling?" Fargo asked.

"Still a little dizzy but much better," Barnaby said.

"Tell her what happened last night," Fargo said and Barnaby focused his eyes on Karen and told her of Clay Sanborn's visit and the gift of the brandy.

"Lucky for Fargo, he didn't drink any of it," Barnaby said. "Because this morning I could just about see and just about stand."

"Your little plan didn't work, honey," Fargo said.

"I'd nothing to do with it," she shot back.

"According to Sanborn, you said I should have an extra drink for you. I'd say that's damn well being part of it. I'd also say that neither of you know how to spell sportsmanship," Fargo said.

"Come with me, dammit," Karen said, spinning on her heel and starting out of the shack.

"No, thanks," Fargo said.

She paused and glared at him. "I came with you. Now you come along with me," she snapped. He considered for a moment and followed her outside where he pulled himself into the saddle. She was already into a canter and he caught up with her, glanced across at her face. She rode tight-lipped, a frown on her brow and he went with her across a low rise, past a well-tended cattle ranch and the white rail fences of a horse farm. She turned onto a road that went westward and he saw the gatepost loom up ahead of him. SANBORN FARM—FINE HORSES the sign on the gatepost read and he followed Karen around a circular pathway to a columned, brick colonial with tall, arched windows, a house of gracious elegance. "You can wait here," she said as she leaped from the horse and strode to the white painted door.

Clay Sanborn stepped out before she had a chance to knock. Karen Bradbury swung before he had a chance to say anything, a stinging slap that landed alongside his cheek. Without a word, she spun and stalked back to her horse and pulled herself into the saddle. Sanborn took a step forward as he rubbed his cheek with his hand. "Dammit, Karen, I did it for you," he said, his voice with more whine than apology in it.

"Don't you ever, ever involve me in anything like that again, Clay Sanborn. I don't like losing, but I won't be a part of that kind of winning," she flung back at him, wheeled her bay around and raced away. Fargo caught up to her outside the gate when she slowed. "You believe me now?" she tossed at him.

"I guess so," he said.

"Then you can see me back to my place," she said and led the way north along the first road they'd taken. When she turned in between two stone gateposts, he saw a modest, low-roofed ranch house and behind it, well-tended, white fences enclosing three corrals where more than a dozen horses idled. He noted two ranch hands moving hay and bags of oats into a freshly painted stable. She halted in front of the house and slid from the saddle. "Come in for a moment," she said.

"Why not?" he said and knew she saw him wince as he dismounted. He followed her into the house and a large living room, well furnished with a leather couch, soft chairs, and the walls hung with paintings of horses as well as some prize ribbons. He watched her move gracefully to a cabinet, take out a bottle of whiskey, and pour two glasses. She handed him one and raised hers in a toast.

"To the victor," she said and sipped from her glass.

"You put on quite an exhibition these past three days, Fargo."

"Proving what the right kind of prize will do for a man," he said.

"I might say thank you, under other circumstances," Karen said.

"No need to. All you have to do is pay up," Fargo said.

"As I said, when I'm ready," she returned.

"Don't take too long to get ready," he said. "A gambling debt is a debt of honor."

"I'm aware of that," she said tartly. "I just proved I know about honor."

"Not completely." Fargo smiled and saw her bristle at once.

"I thought you believed me now," she protested.

"I do, about the brandy. But you weren't above dirty tricks in the race. You worked with Sanborn to try and box me in."

"That wasn't dirty tricks. That was just racing tactics," she said.

"You know better than that, honey," Fargo said and her truculent silence was its own answer. He finished the whiskey and set the glass down. "I'll be going now," he said and saw her light blue eyes studying him thoughtfully.

"You're special. You proved that. It's too bad we can't be friends," she said.

"Maybe we can't be friends, but we're sure going to be friendly." Fargo smiled.

"It'd make a lot of difference to me if you'd stay away from my father's wife," she said as she walked to the door with him.

"Maybe you ought to try and understand her a little more," Fargo said.

"I don't want to understand anyone who cheats on

my father," Karen snapped, blue sparks crackling from her eyes.

"You know, a man I once knew said that a woman was like a river, lots of curves and a soft bottom. But there's another way a woman's like a river. When something dams up its course, it makes another one for itself."

She peered at him for almost a minute, thoughts plainly racing through her mind. "If what you're implying is so, it doesn't change anything for me," she said finally. "There's being faithful. Ever hear of it?"

"There's being understanding. Ever hear of it?" he returned as he climbed onto the Ovaro. "When do I see you next?" he asked.

"At the meeting at my father's place tomorrow night," she said.

"Not exactly what I had in mind," he said and smiled. "See you there."

He made his way back to Barnaby's as the day began to slide to an end and was glad to see the older man step outside. "It's about worn off," Barnaby said. "What'd she want with you?"

"To prove she hadn't been a part of it," Fargo said. "I believe her."

"That's good. Always liked that young woman," Barnaby said.

"I've taken enough of your hospitality, Barnaby. I'll be visiting after the meeting tomorrow night," Fargo said and Barnaby waved to him as he rode on. The night was warm and Fargo bedded down beneath a honey locust. Exhaustion brought instant deep sleep until the new sun finally woke him. His body still ached, especially his breastbone, and he returned to the small lake in the low hills. But this time, instead of the Ovaro benefiting from the soothing water, Fargo undressed and immersed himself in the lake. He spent most of the day in the lake, just standing in water up to his shoulders sometimes, other times floating lazily and occasionally swimming slowly. He spent another hour stretched out in the sun and when it came time to return to town, most of his aches were gone.

Dusk slid over the land as he rode, became night, and he reached Sam Bradbury's house to find almost as many buckboards as horses outside. The front door was open and he entered the large main room where the mayor beckoned to him at once. Fargo's eyes surveyed the men that crowded the room, all of them well dressed with strong faces, men who wore their authority and wealth with belligerent pride. He saw Clay Sanborn, the man's perpetual air of disdain somehow out of place among the others. Sanborn avoided his eyes, he noticed and smiled to himself. He found Karen on the other side of the room, the only woman there, elegantly cool in a tailored, white shirt that rested lightly on the long curve of her breasts. A black riding skirt revealed a nice turn of calf.

"Most everybody knows about you, Fargo, especially after the last three days," Sam Bradbury began. "But I want you to know them. Starting at the left there is Luke Willis. He runs a copper mining operation. Next is Ed Sitwell, cotton farm. Tom Maxwell is in cattle. So's Frank Mullins. Carl Weathers has the biggest horse-breeding farm in the county. You know my daughter, Karen. Stewart Fox, alongside her, has two tobacco plantations at the far end of the plateau. Dave Wright and Herb Stover run a freight line, Max Benson is in cotton, Clay Sanborn in horses, and Harry Anderson has a silver mine."

"I came to hear plans, not introductions," Ed Sitwell called out and Fargo saw the mayor look uncomfortable.

"Every one of these gentlemen have to come to Windsor Bell to get to the bank. Either they're bringing deposits in cash, gold, or silver or they're bringing back payroll monies or loan cash. Having their men robbed and killed is bad enough but, as I told you, we can't get a trail on these damn varmints. That's why I sent for you, Fargo."

"I'm picking up a payroll tomorrow night. Frank Wills agreed to keep the bank open specially for me," Ed Sitwell said. "I haven't been hit yet and I don't want to be. I figured a night pickup might fool them."

"Your plans set?" Fargo queried.

"Yes. That bother you?" the man asked.

"You're giving them a chance to hit and run under the cover of darkness and I'll have to wait till morning. Nobody can pick up a trail in the dark," Fargo said.

Sitwell frowned. "Can't change things now. I still think a night shipment will outfox them."

"We'll see. I'll be there. You won't know it, maybe, but I'll be there," Fargo said.

"It's driving us into the poorhouse," one of the other men said. "We know they head right into the high hills. That's pretty rugged country there but then they disappear."

"So I'm told," Fargo said.

"Now's the time to speak out on anything else on your minds," Sam Bradbury said.

Harry Anderson, the silver miner, stepped forward. "A good lot of us are damn sure who's behind these robberies. We Just haven't been able to prove it. Maybe you'll do that for us," he said.

"Who do you figure's doing it?" Fargo asked.

"The damn valley folks," Anderson said. "Ben Slocum in particular. He's the one they look to for most things."

"Why do you think they're behind it?" Fargo questioned.

"They hate us. They've always hated us," Anderson said. "They'd like to see us go under, all of us. That's coming damn close. Tom lost all the cash he was taking to the bank for his loan payment and Frank lost the cash for two payrolls."

"There's more," Luke Willis said. "Most times those grubbers in the valley can't buy a hammer and nails but suddenly they're all buying new equipment, new wagons, new plow horses. Ben Slocum even bought a fancy Poland China for his hog breeding. Where are they getting all this money all of a sudden?"

An angry murmur of agreement went up from the others and Fargo nodded. "Good question. I'll keep it in mind," he said. "Any more shipments planned for the next few days?"

"I'll be taking a month's receipts to the bank the day after tomorrow. I expect you'll be there," Luke Willis said.

"Count on it," Fargo said.

"Guess that's about it for now," Sam Bradbury announced to bring the meeting to a close. The men quickly filed from the room and Fargo saw Karen leave with Frank Mullins. "I told Ed Sitwell I didn't think much of that night pickup but Ed's a stubborn man," the mayor said.

"Maybe he'll be lucky," Fargo said. "I'll be getting back to you soon as I've something to say." The mayor nodded, his face that of a man tired inside and outside and Fargo walked from the room. He had reached the front door when Libby appeared in the rosy pink housedress. "Thought I'd see you inside," he remarked.

"I don't like crowded, stuffy meetings. I listened

from out here," she said. "You collect on your bet yet?"

"Now, you don't think I'm going to answer that, do you?" Fargo laughed. "That wouldn't be gentlemanly."

Libby studied him a moment longer. "No, you didn't collect yet," she said.

"You seem awfully sure of that," he remarked.

"I'm sure," she said with a satisfied little smile as she strode away. He climbed onto the Ovaro with a wry smile, once again made aware of that singularly accurate intuition that seemed a built-in part of all females. He rode from town, passed the saloon with its hum of voices, and went on to return to the honey locust tree to bed down. He drew sleep to himself at once. The morning would bring a full day, he knew.

5

He circled around the town to arrive at Barnaby's shack where he saw the gray mare saddled and waiting. Barnaby stepped from the shack a moment later. "Going riding?" Fargo inquired. "Good. I came to ask you to come with me."

"I was going to pick some mushrooms down near the river. Some great mycenas grow down there, along with meadow mushrooms, some horse mushrooms too. But that can wait," Barnaby said.

"Thought I'd pay a visit to the valley folks. You said you knew them," Fargo told Barnaby and proceeded to recount what had been said at the meeting.

"They're right about half of it," Barnaby said. "The half about the valley folks hating them." Fargo lifted an eyebrow as they rode over the low hill and the valley spread out in front of them. "Most of the folks in the valley are there because they were pushed, swindled, defrauded, deceived, and just plain cheated by the men at that meeting. Ben Slocum had a piece of that copper mine until Luke Willis swindled him out of it. Ed Sitwell maneuvered Ollie Borne out of the cotton plantation. Jeb Tollman was a partner in Tom Maxwell's cattle ranch before he was jockeyed out of it. I could go on and on. There's hate down there, all right, hate and bitterness and broken men. But I don't know if there's much else," Barnaby said.

"It seems there's suddenly a lot of money going around," Fargo said.

"Yes. I've got to say that takes some explaining," Barnaby admitted.

"Introduce me to Ben Slocum," Fargo said as he turned the pinto down into the valley and Ben led the way to a house almost surrounded by hog pens. The man who stepped from the house wore Levi's and a worn shirt and had a long nose and a long jaw in a dour face.

"Howdy, Barnaby," he said without smiling and Fargo saw eyes that bordered dullness. "Come to visit?"

"Hello, Ben. No, just passing through. This here is Skye Fargo," Barnaby said.

"Saw him at the fair," Ben Slocum said and turned his eyes to Fargo. "You're the feller Sam Bradbury hired to stop the robberies."

"That's right," Fargo said.

"We know what they're saying on the other side of the valley," Ben Slocum said and Fargo saw that a half dozen others had come up to listen, most wearing ragged overalls.

"I don't believe everything I hear," Fargo said, his glance taking in the others who had appeared.

"That's good," Ben Slocum grunted.

"I thought maybe you'd seen something to help me," Fargo said.

"Why would we see anything?" Slocum asked, instant suspicion in his voice.

"You get out of the valley. You've all got eyes," Fargo said.

"Nobody's seen anything. We've nothing to do with the robberies and we don't favor anyone snooping around here to spy on us," Slocum said.

Fargo's eyes hardened. The man was more bluster than threat, he suspected. It was time to back him up a little. "There's spying and there's looking. So far

I'm still looking," he said, his voice suddenly ice and Ben Slocum's belligerence became a truculent glower. Fargo turned the Ovaro in a slow circle and spotted the still spanking clean Studebaker farm wagon in an adjoining field. "Looks brand-new," he commented.

"Any law against havin' a new wagon?" one of the others growled.

"Nope. I'm all for tip-top equipment." Fargo smiled pleasantly. "Be seeing you." He rode slowly away and Barnaby hurried after him, coming up alongside him as he began to ride up the gentle slope leading from the valley. "I'd say they were unfriendly and real defensive," Fargo muttered.

"You're right, but they're pretty much always that way," Barnaby said.

"In other words it doesn't mean a lot," Fargo said.

"It might and it might not," Barnaby said.

"I see three ways to look at this. One, it's one of their own behind it, somebody who wants to see the others go under. Two, it's Ben Slocum's valley folks getting back at the rich landowners who cheated them. Three, it's strictly a real smart outside band of polecats," Fargo said. "I aim to find out which it is."

"I'll help any way I can," Barnaby said.

"Thanks for coming along today," Fargo said as the sun began to lower.

"Good luck tonight," Barnaby called back as he rode on and Fargo turned the Ovaro toward the high hills. The road that bordered the base of the hills was the one Ed Sitwell would use, the most direct route to town from his place. Fargo traversed the road, almost to the town, as he scanned the deep hillsides and made mental notes of the likliest spots an attack might come. He reined up outside of town, backtracked a few dozen yards, and took up a position in a cluster of sycamores, waited as night fell and Ed Sitwell finally appeared. He had two wagons, both one-horse spring wagons with cut-under wheels and six rifle-toting guards on horseback. Fargo made out Sitwell driving with a seventh man sitting beside him.

Staying in the tree cover, Fargo kept pace with the wagons and reined to a halt when they entered town. Still in the trees, he waited for them to begin the trip back with the payroll money from the bank. No attack would come before then. He had just relaxed in the saddle when the sound of gunfire shattered the night, one volley after another, coming from near the center of town. "Shit," Fargo swore as he put the pinto into a gallop and raced into Windsor Bell, down the deserted main street and spotted the two wagons in front of the bank where the lights still burned. He also saw three forms lying still on the ground and one man against a wagon clutching his shoulder. Two more men were ducked behind the wagons, shooting into the darkness and he saw Ed Sitwell push himself out from under one of the wagons as he reined to a halt.

"South, dammit, they went south out of town. They'll turn left and go into the high hills," Sitwell shouted. Fargo raced off, the horse at a full gallop in seconds as it thundered out the other end of town. Fargo saw the high hills rear up to his left and turned, the moonlight affording enough light for him to spot the hoofprints of two horses running side by side into the hills. He reached the hills and sent the pinto up the steep slope, tree and brush instantly darkening the ground and hiding any tracks that might be there. He reined to a halt and strained his ears and caught the faint sound of horses crashing through the brush high into the hills. He swore as he sent the Ovaro upward as he tried to follow the sound. But the densely grown steep hill forced him to be slow or risk the pinto snapping a leg in the blackness. He halted, listened again, but heard nothing this time. They had outdistanced him and he turned the pinto around and made his way down out of the hills.

Sam Bradbury was on the scene when he returned to the center of town, along with what was obviously the town doctor and a burying wagon painted black with closed sides. The three slain men had already been taken from the street and Fargo halted beside Ed Sitwell. "They outfoxed us, dammit. I never expected they'd hit in town," he admitted.

"Just as we were bringing the cash out," Sitwell said. "They got it all and four of my men. They poured shots at us from every damn direction."

"How many were there?"

"Couldn't tell. I'd guess there had to be six," Sitwell said. "The bank had already transferred the money to me so they say it's all my loss, dammit."

"I'll bed down at the edge of town and follow tracks with the first light," Fargo said, "before there's traffic to wipe them out."

"Good luck," Sitwell said, not without bitterness and Fargo rode slowly back to the end of town. He dismounted beneath a tall box elder, slid from the saddle, and sat down with his back against the tree trunk. He managed to sleep after a while, albeit fitfully, and woke when the first gleam of the morning sun crested the high hills. The tracks of four horses were still fresh in the ground, the two he had followed into the hills during the night and two others he hadn't spotted then. The two others broke away and took separate paths up the high slopes and Fargo decided to follow the two that rode together, and as the sun rose higher he saw their hoofprints on the steep slope. He climbed, following the pair of tracks and the slope grew steeper, the hills denser, heavily grown with mountain brush and thick stands of red ash.

The trail of hoofprints led higher and suddenly the steep slope leveled off to become a tree-covered ridge backed by another set of steep hills. The trail divided as the two horsemen had separated, one going right, the other left. Fargo chose to follow the prints that turned left and he saw them swing in closer to the hills that backed the far edge of the ridge. He continued to follow the tracks and then suddenly reined up as he saw the hoofprints double back on themselves. The horseman had reversed his path, then reversed it again until there was only a jumble of unreadable hoof marks. Fargo frowned as he walked the pinto forward and found the place where the horseman had begun to double back and the furrow dug into his brow as he retraced steps. The jumble of prints seemed to end where they tracked over themselves, leading nowhere and Fargo turned to the steep hills and moved the horse along the thick brush. He halted as he spotted the cave, slid from the saddle, the Colt in his hand as he pushed aside brush and found the entrance.

The cave was low-roofed, too low to accommodate a horse, much less a horse and rider and not terribly deep. There was nothing in it but old leaves and the stale odor of weasel and raccoon. Fargo left and walked farther along the face of the hills to halt again but this time at the tall entrance of another cave, partly obscured by two sycamores. He edged his way carefully forward along the side of rock to peer into the caves. It was tall enough and wide enough to hold three or four horses but there was nothing in it and he stepped forward to examine the edges of the cavern. He saw nothing, nothing left from bags or cash, not even hoofprints in dust of the cave floor.

He walked outside and continued to explore the sides of the hill and found another largely hidden cave that seemed entirely unused. Returning to the Ovaro, he decided to follow the hoofprints that had gone to the right. These led halfway around a curve in the grass-covered ridge to where he found two more large caves only a few dozen feet apart. The hoofprints once again doubled back and forth in front of them, seemed to halt and disappear but this time Fargo dismounted and walked to the thick, resilient shrub grass that moved from the hills and down the slope. A horse without the added weight of a rider could be led down the thick, wiry grass and not leave a print. When he turned back to the caves they showed no signs of having been used to hide or store anything, only the remains of small animal bones littering the dankness.

Fargo returned to the Ovaro and rode down the steep slope. He'd find nothing to help him here and when he rode through town he halted at Sam Bradbury's house and the mayor came outside at once. "Find anything?" Bradbury asked.

"I found out somebody's real smart at covering their trail," Fargo said.

"Luke Willis will be taking his receipts to the bank tomorrow. He expects you'll be there," the mayor said.

"I'll start with him," Fargo said and noticed Libby at the window as he rode on. The high hills rose northward at the other end of town and just as steep and dense as south of Windsor Bell. He was tired, having only dozed some during the night but he decided to explore these high hills and sent the horse up a narrow passageway on the steep climb. Sycamore, box elder, and bitternut grew thickly, branches entwining and the Ovaro climbed slowly, its footing unsure until the terrain grew less steep. The hill almost leveled off to a high forest, cool and dark, when he saw the horse and rider materialize through the trees.

"What brings you up here?" Fargo frowned as light blue eyes returned his surprise.

"I come here a lot," Karen said. "I like these high hills. They're mysterious and wild." She wore a red-checked light cotton shirt, the buttons opened enough to show the top of the long curve of her breasts. "I stopped in to see my father. I heard you didn't come up with anything," she said.

"Nothing I liked," Fargo said. "You say you ride up here often. You know where there are any big caves around here?"

"The high hills are full of caves. I can show you four not too far from here," Karen said.

"Show me," he said and she led him to the first cave, well hidden behind a stand of bitternut and plenty large enough to hold three horses. The other caves she showed him were farther along the forest plain where the hills rose in steep, brush-covered cliffs. They, too, were large enough to accommodate horse and rider but like the first one, showed no signs of having been used for anything but bears' dens. The day had grown hot and he heard the sound of a small waterfall and turned the Ovaro toward it. The fall appeared a dozen yards on, the water splashing down a steplike succession of rocks to change into a swift-running mountain stream. But the cool shower of water was too inviting to pass up. He dismounted and began to pull off clothes. "Join me," he suggested as Karen watched from her horse.

"No, thanks," she said coolly and he paused.

"You could kill two birds with one stone," he said. She frowned back. "You could have a refreshing shower and pay off a bet at the same time," he said.

"I'm not in the mood for either," she returned.

"You better start getting in the mood for one, honey," Fargo told her as he peeled off his shirt. She didn't answer but her eyes stayed on him, taking in the smooth, muscled symmetry of his body, he noted. Only when he started to pull off his underdrawers did she turn the bay around and ride slowly away. He smiled as he stretched out in the shower of the waterfall, not at all certain she hadn't stopped to watch from inside the trees. When he felt thoroughly cooled, he stretched out on the grass and let the sun dry him off. The rest of the afternoon he roamed the high hills, found three more large and unused caves and decided both the northern and southern sections of the hills were thoroughly infiltrated with caves.

The day began to slide away when he rode down from the hills, carefully negotiated one of the steeper slopes, and finally reached Windsor Bell where he halted at Sam Bradbury's house. "You know what time Luke Willis plans taking in his receipts tomorrow?" Fargo asked.

"Midafternoon. He stopped by," the mayor said. "I've something else. Arnie Jones bought that new plow he's always been wantin' from Ben Staller today."

The mayor paused to let his words sink in. "Arnie Jones is one of the valley folk," Fargo said.

"That's right. He and Ben Slocum are real close," the mayor said. "Luke Willis and the others are saying it's getting pretty damn plain who's hitting them."

"Maybe they're right, but I'm not jumping to any answers," Fargo said as he left to find Libby just outside the front door.

"Where are you going to be tonight?" she asked.

"Barnaby's probably," he said.

"Shove that. Go to the honey locust," she said.

He hesitated and had to wonder why. No sudden attack of conscience, he felt certain. And Libby was tempting, exuding hungry sexuality. But she could become a complication, the demanding possessiveness still a part of her. He didn't want added complications at this time, he decided. "Not tonight," he said. "Sorry."

"That little bitch get to you with her damn morality?" Libby snapped. "That's all you'll get out of her."

"Nobody's gotten to me with anything," Fargo said and wondered why he was suddenly so angry. He left Libby without a wave back and it was dark when he reached Barnaby's place where Barnaby had enough tasty, marinated venison for him to take dinner. He told Barnaby of Arnie Jones's new plow and the old-timer wore sadness in his face.

"Can't blame the others for what they're thinking. Sure looks that way," Barnaby said.

"And that bothers you," Fargo said.

"It does. Those folks have had enough done to them. I hate to see them bring more trouble onto themselves by this kind of thing," Barnaby said.

"It's not smart," Fargo agreed. "But it may be human. Thanks for supper. I'll be in touch."

"Whatever I can do," Barnaby said and stayed in his chair as Fargo left, swung onto the Ovaro, and rode west toward Luke Willis's place. He found a spot a mile from the man's copper mine and bedded down and slept soundly till the morning came. He washed in a stream, dressed leisurely and it was near noon when he arrived at the mine. Luke Willis greeted him outside a payroll hut. "Good to see you, Fargo," the man said.

"I won't be riding with you," Fargo said and Willis began to protest.

"You have your men to ride payroll. I'm here to put a stop to the robberies. I'll be near. That's all you have to know," Fargo said.

Willis closed his mouth and nodded though not happily. "Have it your way. Just get the job done," he said and retired into the hut. Fargo rode on along a rise that let him look down on the road Willis would take from the mine. It curved and came close to the high hills about a mile on south and Fargo stayed on the high ground as long as he could until it brought him out to the road again. He made his way into a stand of white ash that let him see the road where it curved against the base of the high hills and he positioned himself deep in the trees about two hundred yards from the spot. He searched the far side of the road but saw no sign of horsemen. But the tree cover was dense. They could filter in without being seen, he knew and continued to wait with his lips a grim line. The stand of white ash stretched upward along his side of the road but he kept his concentration on the tree cover on the opposite side.

He had waited about an hour, he guessed, when Luke Willis came into sight on the road. No wagons for Willis, Fargo noted. Six guards and himself, all carrying rifles. Two of the men carried moneybags slung across their saddles while Willis and the others flanked them. They had reached the slow curve in the road when the first volley of shots exploded. Fargo saw two of Willis's men go down as the gunfire erupted from the trees on the other side. "Take cover," he heard Willis shout and the rest of his men started to race toward the white ash on his side of the road when the second volley came, but this one from the white ash.

"Jesus," Fargo swore as the two men with the moneybags on their saddles went down and he saw Luke Willis dive from his horse. They had Willis and his men trapped in a cross fire. Fargo swore again. He hadn't been aware of the attackers who'd taken up positions on his side of the road, but they weren't aware of his presence either. He sent the Ovaro racing back through the ash as he saw four riders race from the other side of the road and seize the moneybags. Others were still firing from the other side and from the white ash on his side, pinning Willis and his remaining two men to the ground. Fargo drew his Colt and raced back and the figures in the white ash came into sight, two men, on foot. They turned as they suddenly heard him coming, tried to bring their rifles to bear, but he fired two shots with but a split second between each and both men flew backward as they went down.

Fargo swerved the Ovaro out of the trees and onto the road just in time to see the four horsemen disappear into the cover on the other side. He charged across the road past Willis who still lay flattened on the ground, raced into the trees on the other side, and heard the riders starting to climb up the steep slopes of the high hills. He sent the Ovaro after them and saw the hoofprints showed they were still riding together. But when the slope grew less steep and finally began to level off the two sets of hoofprints separated, one pair going to the right, the other left. It was the same tactic they had used the last time, he thought as he followed the ones that split right. But it wasn't night and he was a lot closer this time.

The two horsemen he followed swerved, climbed another steep slope and he followed. This time the slope ended in a flat area that butted against tall, almost perpendicular dirt-covered hillsides. Their prints were clear and easy to follow. They led directly to the tall sides of rock and he saw where they had halted for a moment, hoofprints making small circles and then they'd taken off again along the flat area. Fargo galloped in pursuit and saw the two riders had veered right and started down the slopes. He rode recklessly, confident of the Ovaro's power and fleet-footedness and soon he heard the two riders ahead of him. The slope began to level off though the tree cover remained dense, but the Ovaro had a chance to use its skill and swerving at full gallop and it was but a few minutes more when he glimpsed the two horsemen ahead of him.

They heard him, both turning simultaneously and he saw them draw their guns. They fired, wide and too fast, but he flattened himself down across the horse's jet black neck. They had slowed and the Ovaro was coming up fast on them as Fargo drew the big Colt. He wanted at least one alive to give answers but not at the expense of taking a bullet. He swerved the pinto as both men fired another round at him, took aim at one, and fired. The man half spun in the saddle before he flew off sideways. Fargo had hoped the second one might rein up, but the man fired another two shots and raced off. Fargo sent the Ovaro on a parallel path through the trees and came almost abreast of the fleeing horseman. "Pull up and you ride away alive," he shouted.

The man's answer was another shot that came uncomfortably close. Fargo drew abreast of him, aimed low, and fired and saw the man clutch at his thigh with one hand as he cursed in pain. He lost his balance and toppled from the horse and Fargo reined to a halt, turned the Ovaro and walked toward the figure on the ground. The man lay on his side, his leg drawn up in pain, his gun a half dozen feet away on the grass. "Jesus, my leg," the man groaned.

"Your doing. I want some answers. Turn over," Fargo said. He saw the man start to turn and then glimpsed the second gun in his hand. "Damn," Fargo swore as he ducked and the man fired from his position half on his back. The bullet grazed Fargo's hat.

It would have hit on target if he hadn't glimpsed the gun and had the split-second moment to react. The man fired again as Fargo dug heels into the Ovaro and the horse bolted forward. Fargo pulled him up almost instantly, turned, and saw the man trying to bring himself around to fire again. Fargo's Colt barked and the figure shuddered and lay still. "Damfool," Fargo said as he dismounted and went through the man's pockets. He found nothing to identify him and pulled himself back onto the Ovaro. He didn't bother examining the other one, certain he'd find nothing more on him.

He retraced steps, found the spot where the other two riders had gone left, and followed their tracks. They led up another steep slope to where the land leveled again, but only in a half-round circle that butted against high rock and brush. The two riders had gone to the side of rock and halted, he saw, then taken off again. He followed, cursing softly, aware that they'd separate again and he was right as the hoofprints parted midway down the second slope. He reined up. Following farther would be a waste of time, he knew. They had gone their way and somewhere they'd have covered their tracks. He rode slowly back to where the initial attack had taken place with a grudging respect for the attackers. Theirs was a carefully and cleverly planned operation. Today's flight had followed the same pattern as those who'd fled the night before, a pattern designed not only to throw off pursuit but also to leave confusion and frustration.

He found Luke Willis and two of his men waiting amid the slain figures strewn across the road. "I sent back to the mine for a wagon," the man said bitterly. "I don't see you carryin' any moneybags."

"No, you don't. And the two I chased weren't carrying them either," Fargo said.

"Then you chased the wrong two, goddammit," Willis said.

"Maybe and maybe not," Fargo said, grim-lipped. "This is a real smart operation."

"All I know is I'm out a hell of a lot of money," Luke Willis said.

"I'll find out how they're doing it, count on it," Fargo said with more confidence than substance and he turned the Ovaro back into the trees. Slowly this time, he followed the trail of the second two riders up to see if somewhere they had turned off and their trail into the hills taken up by another pair of riders. But he found no signs of that having happened, no place where they even slowed down until they halted against the high rocks. He rested the Ovaro for a few moments as thoughts tumbled in his mind. The first two he had pursued hadn't had the moneybags. Had they dropped them somewhere? Had the second pair had the money? Then why had both pairs raced to the rock walls, halted and then raced away? That could have been part of a tactic to confuse pursuit but somebody had to have had the moneybags.

He turned off thoughts and made his way slowly along the dirt-and-rock cliffs from where he'd halted to where the first pair had stopped. It was halfway between the two points that he came upon the cave entrance, partially hidden by the tall brush. But no hoofprints led to it and he pushed his way through the brush more out of curiosity than hope. The cave was large enough to hide a horse but the thin layer of dust and dirt that covered the stone floor showed only bear and raccoon tracks. He backed from the cave and rode on, found nothing to help him, and rode from the high hills again, this time as the day drew to an end. He thought he owed it to Sam Bradbury to report to him and found the man halfway through a bottle of bourbon.

"I heard," the mayor said. "You don't do any better and I'm out of a job."

"They're not giving me much time, it seems," Fargo said.

"I promised them fast results," the man said.

"That's your fault," Fargo returned.

"They're all hurtin' and I'm the one they can strike back at," Sam Bradbury said.

"Getting rid of you won't stop the attacks," Fargo said.

"They figure they'll bring in somebody who can. That's the way they think," the man said, poured himself another shot of bourbon and drained half of it in one long pull. Fargo turned and walked from the room to find Libby in the foyer.

"He needs some comforting," Fargo said.

"He's getting it," she sniffed.

"You're all heart, aren't you?" Fargo said.

"He's happier with the bottle. It doesn't ask anything of him," she said. She went to the door with him as he stepped outside. "You still playing monk?" she tossed at him.

"For now," he said and she managed not to slam the door as she shut it. He rode through the town to Barnaby's shack to find out again that bad news travels fast.

"What next?" Barnaby asked.

"Everyone points a finger at Ben Slocum and the valley folks. Maybe I can pin that down tomorrow," Fargo said. "One of them has bought something new after every attack. Let's see if that's going to happen again."

"I'd like to come along," Barnaby said. "Bed down here and we can leave together afore sun's up."

"You've a deal," Fargo said and Barnaby sealed it by a hearty dish of leftover venison that tasted as good as it had the first night. Fargo slept in the little half room and woke a half hour before dawn and heard Barnaby brewing coffee in the other room. He dressed, shared a mug of the hot, bracing brew, and rode off in the predawn blackness with Barnaby beside him.

"I hope this pays off for you but I'll be sorry if it does," Barnaby said. "Figure you'll understand that."

"I do," Fargo said. "It's called mixed feelings. I've got some myself, but different." Barnaby threw him a questioning glance but Fargo decided against explaining further as the first gray light of dawn appeared and the valley stretched out below them.

6

Fargo had taken up a position in a stand of shagbark hickory that let him look directly across at Ben Slocum's place. He sat motionless, Barnaby beside him, as the morning sun rose higher. The door of the house opened minutes after the sun began to flood the valley and Ben Slocum emerged. He crossed in front of the house and walked to the edge of the valley across a field to where a line of tall beggarweeds mixed in with wild geraniums to form a kind of hedgerow. He walked along the hedgerow, came to the middle of it and reached into the cluster of wild geraniums. He seemed to be groping through the bushes, searching and when his hand came out it was holding something.

Fargo peered hard before his voice came, a whispered sound. "That's one of Luke Willis's moneybags," he said. Barnaby made no reply but Fargo heard the long sigh escape him. He watched Ben Slocum cross back over the field with the moneybag and hurry into his house. He emerged a minute later and began to hurry toward the line of tattered houses that lay beyond his in the valley. When he paused at the door of the first one and then stepped inside, Fargo sent the Ovaro out of the trees. "Let's go," he said to Barnaby as he crossed the space to Ben Slocum's house. "Stay here," he told Barnaby as he entered the house, paused, and heard the sounds of others waking in the back room, a woman's voice talking to youngsters. The moneybag was in the center of the floor and Fargo took one long step, scooped it up, and slipped from the house with it. He climbed onto the Ovaro and stuffed the moneybag into his saddlebag where it made a sizable bulge. He beckoned to Barnaby to follow as he hurried the Ovaro back into the trees where he halted and turned to look out into the valley again.

Ben Slocum emerged from the house with another man and both hurried to an adjoining house. They made hurried stops at five more houses and then all began to return to Ben Slocum's place, seven in all, hurrying with long, eager strides. The others halted while Ben Slocum went into his house and Fargo nodded at Barnaby and pushed the Ovaro out of the trees. He walked the horse toward the knot of men and had almost reached them when Ben Slocum burst from the house. "It's gone," he heard the man cry out. "I thought maybe Mary moved it but she told me no." Ben Slocum looked up and saw Fargo approaching, Barnaby a step behind him.

" 'Morning," Fargo said. "Something wrong? You look white as a piece of cotton ticking."

"I lost something, that's all," Ben Slocum said. "You see anybody leave the valley?"

"Nope. What did you lose?" he inquired casually.

"Just something I wanted," Ben Slocum said, irritation in his voice.

"Could this be it?" Fargo asked and pulled the bag from his saddlebag. Ben Slocum stared at him, his mouth falling open and the others looked at Fargo, then at Ben Slocum and back to Fargo. "We watched you take it out of the hedgerow," Fargo said. "It's time for you to start talking." His eyes swept the others with a hard glance. "Don't anybody try anything foolish," he said.

"No, sir. Most of us were at the fair. We saw you shoot," one man said and Fargo returned his eyes to Ben Slocum.

"We didn't steal it," the man said. "We didn't do any of those attacks, honest we didn't. That there moneybag was left for us."

"And there's been one left for you after every robbery," Fargo said.

"That's right." Slocum nodded vigorously and was joined by a muttered chorus of agreement from the others.

"Who leaves it?" Fargo asked.

"We don't know," Slocum said.

"How do you know where to look?" Fargo pressed.

"There was a note left under my door after the first robbery. It told me where to look," Slocum said. "I began looking after each robbery and there was always somethin' there, a bundle of bills, a moneybag, a sack of gold, something. We decided to divide it up each time."

"You're asking for a lot of believing, Ben," Barnaby put in.

"Guess so," Slocum said. "But it's true, every word of it."

"No matter, it still makes you part of it," Fargo said. "You damn well knew it wasn't yours."

"Findin' ain't the same as robbin'," the man protested.

"Then why didn't you turn it in to the mayor?" Fargo speared.

The men exchanged uncomfortable glances and it was Ben Slocum who finally spoke. "Never look a gift horse in the mouth," he said. Fargo kept his face expressionless but he knew the answer was one that most men would share.

"And we figured it rightly was ours, seein' as how

103

they cheated and swindled most of us," another man added.

"Well, the free ride is over. I'm taking this to Sam Bradbury," Fargo said, touching the moneybag.

"He'll arrest us. He won't believe us, none of them will," Slocum said.

"You're right there," Fargo agreed. "I'm not saying I believe any of you, either, but for now, I'm going to tell Sam Bradbury I found the moneybag, that one of the bandits must've dropped it. But I find out that it really has been you, I'm coming back for you, you can count on it." Slocum and the others nodded, their faces grave. Fargo wheeled the pinto around and paused as he swept the men with a hard glance. "You do any more finding you turn it in," he ordered and they nodded.

He put the horse into a trot and rode away, then slowed as Barnaby caught up to him as they climbed from the valley. "You're giving them the benefit of the doubt," Barnaby said. "You're either mighty understanding or you're giving them enough rope to hang themselves."

Fargo laughed. "Maybe a little of both and maybe something else," he said.

"Such as?" Barnaby queried.

"I don't think they're smart enough to have planned this operation. I won't write them off, but this is a real smart deal, from the attacks to the getaways. Hell, they weren't smart enough to keep themselves from being cheated and swindled. Going on a spending spree after each robbery was pretty dumb, too."

"Well, if they're telling the truth about the money being left for them each time, what does that mean? We've got some Robin Hood running around robbing the rich to give to the poor?" Barnaby frowned.

"It could be, or it could be somebody who wants it

to look like that. But it sure puts a new twist on things," Fargo said.

"Where do you go from here?" Barnaby asked.

"Two can play at being smart," Fargo said.

"Fill me in when you're ready," Barnaby said.

"When I'm ready." Fargo nodded and the older man rode on as Fargo turned to make his way slowly along the well-tended houses and farms. He saw Clay Sanborn as he passed his place, the man working a young horse in one of the corrals. Sanborn saw him and looked away and Fargo rode on. He had neared the last of the wealthy homes when the slender rider on the bay came down the road.

"Visiting?" Karen asked.

"Passing by. Just came from the valley," Fargo said.

Her eyebrows lifted a fraction. "Getting closer to the answer?" she remarked.

"Maybe," he said noncommittally. "Maybe I was on my way to visit you."

"You thirsting? Don't tell me little Libby hasn't been taking care of you or vice versa," she said, a cool, taunting smile edging her lips.

"That's not your concern, honey," Fargo said quietly.

"The hell it isn't," she snapped.

"The hell it is," he returned. "You lost a bet, remember? That's your concern, nothing else."

The cool smile disappeared. "I can't turn off the way I feel," she said, frowning.

"You can't turn off paying up, either," Fargo told her.

"All right, soon," she muttered.

"You're close to the end of your rope," Fargo said.

"I'll remember that," she said and sounded suddenly contrite. She was changeable as all hell or a damn good actress. He wasn't sure which, he mused. He nodded to her as she moved the big bay on, riding smoothly, her longish breasts hardly swaying, her willow-wand figure entirely in rhythm with the horse. He turned and rode on until he reached town and the mayor's house.

Sam Bradbury's eyes showed the effects of too much whiskey even though he was sober. "When's the next shipment to the bank?" Fargo asked.

"Tomorrow. Harry Anderson's bringing in a shipment of silver, his month's mining," the mayor said.

"It's common knowledge, right?" Fargo queried.

"He brings it same day every month. I know he was thinking of changing it. He'll be stopping by soon. We all agreed every shipment has to be cleared with me," Bradbury said.

"Tell him to prepare to go on as usual," Fargo said.

"If this goes wrong too, it'll be my neck for sure," the man said.

"I don't imagine they'll be too happy with me either," Fargo said.

"Hell, you can just ride off. You've been paid. For me it's the end. I'm too old to start over and there's not much call for ex-mayors," Sam Bradbury said.

"Just tell Anderson to go on with his shipment," Fargo said. "By the way, where is his place exactly?"

"At the far end of the plateau, in front of the hills where he does his silver mining," Bradbury said and Fargo left him to climb onto the Ovaro, glad to have missed a meeting with Libby. The day ended and he stopped at the saloon for a drink and a buffalo sandwich, turned down two offers from the best-looking of the girls and when the night grew deeper he left and rode back to the plateau, past the mostly darkened homes and empty corrals. He saw the gleam of a light still on at Karen's place but kept going and finally saw the bare hills rising up, outlined by a pale moon. The long, low house in front of them was dark and still as Fargo dismounted and knocked on the door. He had to knock three times before he caught the sound of footsteps from inside.

"Who is it?" the voice asked.

"Fargo," he said, heard the latchbolt slide back and Harry Anderson opened the door, a heavy Remington in his hand, a nightshirt clothing his body.

"Jesus, you know what time it is?" the man muttered.

"I know. I want to talk to you," Fargo said and the silver miner opened the door for him to step inside. He lighted a lamp and carried it into the living room as Fargo followed. "What the hell is all this about, Fargo?" he said with a frown.

"It's about outfoxing the fox," Fargo said. "Where's the silver you'll be shipping to the bank tomorrow?"

"Here in my safe where I always keep it, all in sacks ready to go," Anderson said.

"Take it out of the sacks and keep it in your safe," Fargo said. "We're going to put rocks in the sacks instead. You've got to have a lot of rocks out back."

"Sure," Anderson said.

"Now listen carefully and tomorrow you'll do exactly what I tell you now," Fargo said. "No one's going to know about this but you and me. Your men are going to think they're carrying the silver in those sacks. You'll take the road that edges the high hills."

"You figure they'll hit us and get only sacks of rocks," Anderson said, his eyes taking on brightness.

"That's right and they'll go with it the way they have each time. Only this time I'm going to be waiting in the high hills," Fargo said. "But there's one more thing. You tell your men not to try to fight back. Tell them they're to hit the dirt at the first shot and crawl for cover. I don't want men getting killed over a shipment of rocks."

"Fair enough," Anderson said. "Now let's get those rocks." Not bothering to change out of his nightshirt, he hurried out the back door and Fargo followed. They made three trips with the rocks and then Harry Anderson opened an old iron safe in a study and they transferred the rocks for the silver in the sacks. "There, that does it," the man said when they finished, the nuggets of silver pushed into the rear of the safe behind the sacks.

"When can I ship the real silver?" Anderson asked. "The bank uses it to cover the cash they pay my suppliers. I don't get that silver there, they don't pay and I don't have any supplies."

"If it goes well, you can ship in a day or two," Fargo said.

"And if it doesn't?"

"I might need a few more days but I expect I'll be close to wrapping it up after tomorrow," Fargo said.

"Everybody will like hearing that," Anderson said as he walked to the door with Fargo.

"You just carry through your part tomorrow," Fargo said and rode into the night. He circled under the pale moon and made his way up into the high hills. The heavy tree cover made it too black to go on and he bedded down under a bitternut and slept until dawn filtered its way through the trees. He rose, found a cluster of blackberries on which to breakfast, and rode higher, almost to where the slope leveled off to become the ridge that butted against the tall rocks. This was where the bandits had ridden at least twice, probably every time, only to unexplainably ride away. They would do so again, he was certain, but this time he'd have the answers he wanted.

He secured a spot in the trees and began the wait, relaxed, confident. He was too high to see or hear the attack on the road but that was unimportant now.

Waiting, being ready, that was the important thing. The sun rose higher, filtered through the trees more strongly and he passed the time watching the Baltimore orioles sweep through the trees, brilliant flashes of orange and black. The sun was directly overhead he saw through the trees when his ears caught the sound from below, brush being pushed aside, then the soft thud of horses climbing upward. He held his place, peered through the trees and the riders came into sight, two again, each carrying Harry Anderson's sacks slung onto their saddle horns.

They rode past him, some fifty yards away through the trees and he turned the Ovaro to watch them climb onto the ridge where the slope leveled off. He had to move upward to keep them in sight, saw them race to the tall dirt and rock formation, rein to a halt, circle and then drop the sacks on the ground. Instantly they turned and began to race down the hillside and Fargo's lips drew back in a grimace. He could wait to see who picked up the sacks but they mightn't be picked up for hours. Or perhaps not at all. They were clever enough for that and there was another pair of riders with sacks not too far away. But he had the two riders in front of him. A bird in hand is worth two in the bush, he decided and sent the Ovaro downhill at an angle. There was no chance to creep up on his quarry in silence and the two men turned as they heard him coming.

They separated at once and Fargo took after the nearest one. He didn't want a repeat of what happened the last time and he'd planned to stop that. The rider drew his gun and fired as Fargo closed ground. But Fargo didn't yank his Colt out. Instead, he closed further, flattened himself low as the man fired again, two shots this time. Three altogether so far, Fargo counted and kept the Ovaro closing in. The rider swerved, slowed, and fired again. Four, Fargo counted as the bullet passed too close. But he kept closing and swung himself over the side of the horse, clinging onto the saddle horn with one hand, one foot still in the stirrup as the man fired again. The shot flew across the seat of the saddle and the Ovaro was almost abreast of the other horse. Fargo lifted his head a fraction and saw the man fire again, the shot wild this time.

Six, Fargo muttered as he pulled himself back into the saddle. The man was frantically trying to reload without losing speed as Fargo brought the lariat up, sent it in a long arc and saw the loop close over the man's shoulders. He yanked as he reined up and the man flew from his horse and landed hard on the ground. Fargo leaped down, pulled on the lariat again, and flipped the man onto his back as the gun fell to the ground. Fargo kicked it away, released his grip on the lariat, and pulled the man to his knees. "Talk fast. I'm short on patience," Fargo rasped.

"I don't know anything," the man said.

Fargo drew his Colt and pushed it into the man's face. "Don't even try bullshitting me, Mister," he said.

The man's face drained of color and his eyes bulged. He had a narrow face with no character in it and blue veins stood out on his temple. "I don't know anything," he said hoarsely and Fargo saw only abject fear in his face. He pulled the Colt back.

"Tell me what you *do* know," he said.

"I'm hired. Me and the others, and we're told to bring the money or the sacks up here," the man said.

"Who hired you?" Fargo questioned.

"Tim Halligan," the man said. "He hired all of us."

"Who hired Tim Halligan?" Fargo asked.

"I don't know. None of us do. He's the only one

who knows that. We never see anybody but him," the man said.

"He come along on the raids?"

"No. We have our orders and we carry 'em out," the man said. Fargo grunted silently. Smart, another example of it. Anyone caught knew nothing, the real brains twice removed.

"Halligan pick up the bags?" Fargo asked.

"No," the man said.

"Then we'll start with him. You'll take me to him," Fargo said.

"I can't do that. He'll kill me," the man said.

"I'll kill you if you don't," Fargo said. "Your choice."

"Not much of a choice," the man muttered. Fargo pulled him to his feet as he kept the lariat around him.

"Get on your horse. We'll pick up the bags, first," Fargo said and let enough slack in the rope for the man to mount and ride in front of him up the slope. Fargo curved to the left and finally reached the ridge and the spot where the men had dropped the bags. They were gone. "I'll be dammed," he swore as his eyes swept the ground. No new hoofprints, only those that had been made by the two riders. He brought his eyes to scan the rock and brush wall. There was no cave opening anywhere near. He scanned the ground for new hoofprints again but there were none. "I'll be damned," he said again. Tim Halligan was suddenly the key, the link that could tie it all together.

Fargo, holding the end of the lariat, felt the sudden pull on the rope. He spun to see the man pull the revolver from his saddlebag. Fargo cursed as he drew the Colt, his hand moving with the speed of a cougar's strike. "No, don't," he shouted but the man raised the pistol to fire. Fargo cursed again as his finger pressed the trigger and the Colt barked. The man's shot went wild as his chest erupted in a shower of red and he toppled backward from his horse. Fargo's long sigh was part anger and part frustration. The line to Tom Halligan was erased. The link in the chain had been snapped. He pulled the lariat from around the man's shoulders and returned it to the lariat strap on his saddle and sent the pinto downhill.

It hadn't been a total loss. He had learned the meaning of the hoofprints that went nowhere and doubled back on themselves. They didn't take refuge in caves and they didn't hide their loot in caves. They left it for someone to pick up, but that other horseman still managed to disappear without hoofprints. That question still shimmered without an answer. However this time he'd not be the only one frustrated. Someone would discover they had only worthless rocks and he took satisfaction in that. He'd take comfort wherever he found it these days. When he finally reached the road at the base of the high hills he found Harry Anderson still there with one of his men. "I sent the others back with the wagon," Anderson said.

"Anyone hurt?" Fargo inquired.

"No," Anderson said. "You get them?"

"Close but no bull's-eye. Learned a few things though, enough to add to the picture. And we won in a way. You didn't lose a nugget."

"That makes me happy," Anderson said. "When do I send the real shipment through?"

"By next week. I want some time to follow through on some leads," Fargo said.

"Can't wait longer than that. Got to get that silver into the bank or I'm in real trouble," Anderson said as he rode off, his man following. Fargo turned south, reached town, and stopped at the mayor's where he told Sam Bradbury what had succeeded and what hadn't.

"You still don't know who's doing it. You don't have a real lead," the mayor said.

"No, but I've a lot more of the pieces. That'll help me get the rest of it," Fargo said and saw that Sam Bradbury had grown afraid to hope. He walked from the room and Libby met him in the hall, her eyes searching his face and then a smug smile crossing her own round-cheeked countenance.

"Time for exchanging, Fargo," she said.

His eyes narrowed at her. "Keep talking."

"You've something I want, damn you. I'm burning up for you. Now I've something you'll want to hear. Exchanging," Libby said. "I'll come to that honey locust tonight. Be there."

She was being demanding, on purpose, well aware he'd hate that, he realized. And enjoying every moment of it. But she was holding onto something. It was there in the craftiness of her eyes. "Never turn down an invitation, 'specially one put so sweetly," he said and saw the satisfaction flood her face as he brushed past her and returned to the Ovaro. Dusk had slipped over the town and darkness by the time he reached Barnaby's shack.

"You didn't get what you wanted to get but neither did they," Barnaby said when he finished.

"I might have something more tomorrow," Fargo said.

"Stop by when you do." Barnaby nodded and Fargo rode his way from town, made a slow circle, and returned to the honey locust. He laid out his bedroll and sat on it as he chewed a piece of cold beef jerky from his saddlebag. The moon had begun to move farther across the blue velvet sky when he saw the horse and rider approach at a slow walk, take shape,

113

and become Libby. She wore the long, rosy pink housedress and her deep breasts bounced as she slid from the saddle. Her hands reached up and she began to unbutton his shirt, then his Levi's.

"You said exchanging," he reminded her.

"After. Don't be suspicious. It's not becoming," she said and pulled his Levi's down. She sank to her knees as he kicked off clothes and pulled the buttons of the housedress open. She was clasping him, making growling eager little sounds as she fell onto the sleeping bag with him, caressing, kissing, pulling on him, rubbing her face up and down his throbbing warmth. Again there were no preliminaries with Libby, no rising to passion's heights. The heights were there instantly, exploding, demanding, compelling in their intensity and he felt himself carried upward with her, matching her unvarnished hungering, thrust for thrust, groan for groan, harshness for harshness.

Finally her scream exploded, tore at the night and her deep, pillow breasts filled his mouth until she fell away and lay beside him, deep gasps fighting up from her lips. "Jesus, that was great. You're a damn drug," she murmured.

"You're your own drug, Libby," he said, not ungently.

She turned a thoughtful glance at him. "Maybe," she said.

"I'm here tonight because I thought it was what I ought to do for you. I'm not convinced you've any real exchanging to do," Fargo said.

"But I do," Libby said as she sat up and let him enjoy the lushness of her compact body. "It's about Clay Sanborn."

"What about Clay Sanborn?" Fargo asked at once.

"He's lent money to most everyone, giving them all loans they need because of the robberies and which the bank wouldn't give them. He's taken deeds to their stock, lands, and business for the loans. If they go under, Clay Sanborn will own damn near everything."

Her words shimmered. "Where'd you hear this?" he asked.

"Clara Mullins. Clara likes her rye and when we visit her tongue gets real loose. Besides, she's worried. Frank Mullins put all his stock up to get his loan from Clay, right down to the last steer." A tiny satisfied smile crossed Libby's face. "That exchanging enough for you?" she slid at him.

"It is," he said as the implication in her words revolved through his mind. Clay Sanborn had suddenly taken on a new role. He had a vested interest in seeing everyone else go down. Had he engineered that happening, Fargo wondered. Or was he just an opportunist standing by and waiting? Fargo couldn't dismiss the possibility but he couldn't embrace it, either. Sanborn was too arrogant to stand by waiting and he was clever enough to have conceived the operation. He was also on the spot, aware of who was shipping what, where, and when. He was on the inside. He fitted—very well.

Fargo's thoughts broke off as Libby rose and stepped into the long housedress. "I'll be going now," she said. "Sam's been sleeping poorly. He'll be up before dawn, wandering around the house. I'd best be there."

Fargo nodded and helped her onto her horse. She rode off, the satisfied smile still touching her face and he returned to his bedroll and stretched out. Before he drew sleep to himself he added new plans to those he already had made for the morning. The night passed quietly and he slept soundly. Libby could do that for a man and when he woke the morning sun was over the tops of the high hills. He washed in a stream, dressed, and found a stand of peaches on which to breakfast. He put off visiting Barnaby to ride along the well-tended acres of horse and cattle farms and slowed as he reached Clay Sanborn's place. A riding crop in one hand, his perpetual air of disdain wreathing his handsome face, Sanborn stepped through a corral gate toward him as Fargo reined to a halt. "I expected you'd be coming around one of these days," Sanborn said.

"You did?" Fargo said.

"You're not the kind to let go of things," Sanborn said. "You'll insist on your pound of flesh, the mark of a small mind."

"Maybe, but you're right, I still owe you. I'm not here for that though," Fargo said and thought he saw a flash of relief behind the man's mask of disdain. "I'm curious about something. You've a sizable payroll, oats to buy, equipment to replace. Don't you ship any cash to the bank or bring any back?"

"Of course I do," Sanborn said.

"Then I guess you're one of the lucky ones."

"How do you mean that?" Sanborn frowned.

"You're one of the few around here who haven't been hit by the bandits," Fargo said. "Lucky, right?"

"That's the right word," Sanborn said. "But you make it sound as if there's something wrong in being lucky."

"No, just checking out things, earning my pay," Fargo said.

Clay Sanborn's smile was acid, but he showed nothing else. But that was no surprise. He was smart, cool, and immoral. He'd proven that during the contests. "Good," Sanborn said and stepped back into the corral.

Fargo slowly rode on, circled, and made his way back to Barnaby's shack to find the older man outside chopping firewood. Fargo had decided he'd tell Barnaby what he'd learned from Libby but no one else, not even Sam Bradbury and when he finished, Barnaby emitted a low whistle. "That gives a backseat to Ben Slocum, but what about the bags left for him? Sanborn's not the type to play Robin Hood," Barnaby said.

"No, he sure isn't. That doesn't fit, not yet anyway. But it still means that Sanborn will take more watching," Fargo said.

"I've something for you. Karen Bradbury stopped here this morning looking for you. I told her she might find you by that honey locust near the river, but she came back and said you weren't there."

"I was with Sanborn," Fargo said.

"She told me to tell you to come visiting at her place tonight," Barnaby said.

Fargo smiled at the unsaid that hung in Barnaby's voice. "Don't jump to conclusions, not with her," he said.

"I'm just the messenger," Barnaby said blandly as Fargo rode off with a wave. Fargo took the horse back into town and reined up in front of the saloon. There'd be a few customers, of course, there always were at any time of the day or night, but the bartender would have time to talk and that's what he wanted. The possibility of a very clever, completely outside group still existed. Maybe he could cross that off. He had to try and see and he strolled into the saloon to see only a half dozen men at the bar and one girl lounging at one of the tables.

The bartender nodded to him as he approached. "Bourbon," Fargo said.

"On the house," the man said. "You've earned it by that show you put on at the fair, Mister."

"Much obliged," Fargo said, taking a sip of the

drink. "Came by to ask about a man, name of Tim Halligan. Ever hear of him?"

"Tim Halligan," the bartender echoed as he frowned in thought. "Tall, thin, sharp face?"

"I don't know," Fargo said.

"There was a Tim Halligan, worked for Frank Mullins for a while until Frank fired him. Then he worked for Tom Maxwell until Tom fired him. He got a job with Clay Sanborn, then with Karen Bradbury and Ed Sitwell. But they all let him go," the bartender said.

"Why?" Fargo asked.

"Heard he was a good hand but he always wanted to do things his way, couldn't get along with the other men, strictly a loner," the bartender said.

"Thanks a lot," Fargo said as he finished the bourbon, hurried outside, and swung onto the pinto with his brow creased in a deep furrow. A new factor had been added, a man who bore a grudge against everyone who had fired him, all their associates too. Tim Halligan had worked for damn near everyone. He knew movements, patterns, ways, and times. He knew the land. And he had the oldest motive in the world, revenge.

But the man he'd caught had said Tim Halligan didn't pick up the bags. He'd been definite in saying that someone else was behind Halligan, whoever picked up the loot and was the real brains behind everything. But what if the man had been wrong, Fargo asked himself as he rode from town. What if there really was no one behind Tim Halligan? Maybe Halligan was smart enough to make it look that way to the others? Then his assumption had also been wrong, Fargo pondered. But then what if the man had been right? Maybe there was someone behind Halligan. Dammit, Fargo swore, there were too many maybes about everything. Finding Halligan could supply the answers. He'd make that the first priority come morning, he vowed as he rode the Ovaro through the new night and turned toward the plateau.

He didn't hurry, paused to down a stick of beef jerky, and let the night draw on a little further before he arrived at Karen's place. She opened the door as he dismounted, clothed in a yellow gown, silky and smooth. "Expected you'd be here before this," she said as he entered a room where only one lamp burned low.

"I imagine you did. I imagine you expect I'll be happy as a pig in mud that you're ready to pay up," he said.

"I wouldn't phrase it with such delicacy," she sniffed.

He took a step forward, reached out, and pulled her to him and felt the warmth of her breasts through the silky gown. His mouth pressed down on hers, lingered and then he stepped away and saw the banked fire in the light blue eyes, her lips still parted. "You're paid up, honey," he said. "Sleep tight."

He turned and started for the door when her voice speared into him. "Don't you dare," she said and he halted. Her eyes held no banked fire now but shot out shards of light blue flame.

"Dare what?" he asked blandly.

"Insult me," she snapped.

"Now how am I doing that?" he asked.

"It's an insult to refuse payment of a debt of honor. You damn well know that," she shot back. "I refuse to be refused."

He smiled. "And I refuse going through the motions," he said.

He saw her eyes darken and her tongue touched the finely edged lips for an instant. "Maybe it wouldn't be that," she said.

"Prove it," he said. She stepped forward, the light blue eyes suddenly smoldering as her arms lifted to encircle his neck and her lips pressed his, soft and moist, and little quiverings in their touch. The tip of her tongue darted out and drew back at once.

"Proof enough?" she murmured.

"For starters," he said and she took his hand and led him into an adjoining room where two long candles provided the soft light and a pink-sheeted double bed took up most of the space. She turned to him and her hands unbuttoned his shirt slowly with deliberate movements and then slid across his bare chest with the same slowness. He undid his gunbelt, let it fall to the floor as she continued to enjoy the tactile sensation of her palms against his muscled torso. He let his Levi's follow the gunbelt to the floor and then pulled on the little piece of ribbon at the top of the yellow dress. It came open and the dress parted. Karen wriggled her shoulders and the silky garment slid smoothly from her.

He pressed her back onto the bed and stared down at her willow-wand, naked figure—slender loveliness, nice shoulders, and creamy white skin, the longish breasts a lovely slow line, well-cupped at the bottoms and each tipped by the palest of pale pink nipples on equally pale pink areolas. Below the pale pink tips a slender ribcage narrowed to a slender waist, narrow hips and a flat belly, and beneath it, a small but very black little bush, made more striking against the creamy skin, all of it contained and puffed up in one spot. Long, nicely curved thighs just avoided being too thin, but she held them together to one side with girlish gracefulness.

Her light blue eyes were definitely smoldering now, he saw, and her mouth was parted, a waiting in her face and he let his hand move across the longish breasts, touching gently, his thumb passing across one pale pink nipple and her gasp was instant and her hands dug into his back. He stroked again, slowly, and a slow, hissing gasp came again and when he put his lips onto one pale tip she gave a short cry and he felt her body jerk. He pulled on it gently, caressed the edges with his tongue and felt it grow firm in his mouth, his tongue over the very tip touching the faint quiver of it. "Oh, God," he heard Karen whisper, and her hands were sliding up and down his back, touching his buttocks, moving up again, pressing hard against him.

His hand wandered slowly downward, exploring its own warm path as he continued to hold one breast in his mouth and Karen's long slender body trembled, trembled more strongly as his fingers caressed the tiny indentation of her belly and moved down to push through the small, puffed, wiry-smooth nap. He pressed down on a small pubic mound that had lifted, thickened, and he saw Karen's thighs, still pressed together, moving from one side to the other. He sucked on the nipple, drew it upward and she half screamed. "Oh, my God, oh, God . . . oh, yes, oh, yes," her voice came, rose, fell back to a low, hissing gasp.

One hand came behind his neck, pressed him down onto her breasts and she half rolled back and forth to rub her long curved breasts against his face. His hand slid through the puffed-up little nap, touched below it and felt the dampness of her and she half screamed as he touched the very edge of her soft, moist foramen. His hand edged lower, pressed the softness and her legs drew up, still with thighs together, a protective reaction. He let his hand slide in between her thighs, her skin damp, gently pressed further and felt the stiffness go out of her slender thighs. His hand moved, upward, to the black-capped apex, pressed deeper and as she groaned, her thighs fell open. "God, yes . . . oh, yes," her voice came, almost inaudible and his hand pressed the warm moistness of her, touched the quivering lips, caressed, and Karen Bradbury's long, slender legs flew back and forth, opening and closing, welcoming and protesting and welcoming again.

His hand slid deeper as his tongue caressed one pale pink nipple and Karen screamed, a low cry, rising as he caressed her dark depths, "Oh, yes, yes, oh more . . . oh, God more," she breathed and her hands were digging into his back, pulling at him as he moved his pulsating erectness over her, pressed down into the puff-black nap and she cried out at his touch as her slender legs rose up, pressed into his sides. "Please, please . . . slow, slow . . . oh, please," she said and he heard the note of fear in her wanting. He moved, found the wet, waiting aperture and rested his throbbing against it and Karen screamed as her breasts lifted, pressed against his mouth.

He slid forward, slowly, felt the warm smooth tightness around him, continued to move gently and Karen was calling out sounds, no words, just sounds and her long, willowy body began to move with him, sliding forward and back, a slow, sinuous motion, torso, hips, breasts, all moving in unison. "Oooooh . . . oooh . . . aaaaaah . . ." Karen sighed, each long sigh matching her movement and now her slender thighs were rubbing up and down against his sides. He drew back slow, almost from her and her voice rose in an instant cry of protest to become a low moaning sound as he slid forward again. She moved with him with such slow sinuousness that the change took him by surprise with its abruptness.

She began to stiffen, tremble, all the sinuousness vanished, her hips lifting as she stiffened. Her voice rose, became a scream. "Oh, God, oh, God, oh, God, oh, oh, oh," she cried out and he felt the contractions of her around him, demanding, exciting and his own throbbing urges were swept along with her. Her hands dug into his back as her trembling exploded, her long willow body wrapping itself around him as she shivered and shook and gasped sounds of overwhelming ecstasy tore from her. He exploded with her and she cried out as she clung, stayed, pressed every bit of her creamy flesh against him, her arms clasping him so tightly they left marks on his skin. Just as abruptly, she fell away from him and lay on her back, dark brown hair against the pink sheets as she made tiny, almost whimpering sounds. "So good . . . so good . . ." he heard her murmur and he lay down half over her and her slender legs rose to slide around his buttocks.

"It was close to new for you, wasn't it?" he said.

"Let's say it's been a long time," she returned and rose up on one elbow, the palest of pale pink nipples still standing erect. "More than going through the motions?" she asked smugly.

"Much more." He smiled.

"Stay the night," she said, pressing her mouth on his. "I've come to like this paying off bets."

"Good," he said and she curled against him and slept. She woke before the day and he felt her hands, exploring, caressing, arousing and suddenly he was very much awake and the room again echoed with her cries and moans until her ecstasies finally trailed away in his arms. She slept heavily afterward, until he woke with the first light of dawn and slid from beside her and she came awake. She sat up, her willow-wand figure beautifully graceful. "I think I'd best be on my way before everyone is up and about and sees me leaving," he said.

"What if I told you I didn't care?" She smiled.

"I'm not sure I'd believe you." He laughed as he finished dressing and paused to sit on the edge of the bed. "But there is something you can tell me. A man named Tim Halligan worked for you. Do you know where he is now?"

"Tim Halligan? Yes, I fired him. What would you want with him?" Karen frowned.

"I think he's the answer to what's been happening," Fargo said and Karen's frown deepened.

"Tim Halligan? Never," she scoffed.

"Then he can tell me who is. He's the key to it," Fargo said. "You know where he might be?"

"No. He just left. I don't know where he went," Karen said. "He worked for a lot of people here."

"I know. I'll be asking them too," Fargo said.

"You're wasting your time on him," she said.

"I don't think so," Fargo said and started for the door. She unfolded herself from the bed and pressed herself against him, lovely, enticing, naked, and warm. "Don't make this the only visit," she said.

"Count on it," he said as he hurried from the house while he could still cling to his willpower.

7

He had just turned the horse onto the main road past Karen's place when he saw the cluster of men on horseback and the two buckboards. They all turned to him as he rode up and he saw almost everyone who'd been at the meeting at the mayor's house. "We were looking for you," Frank Mullins said and there was accusation in his tone. "They hit Harry Anderson last night, at home, cleaned him out of all that silver he didn't ship the other day."

Fargo felt the surprise stab into him. "Cleaned him out?" he echoed.

"Made him open the safe. Four burst in on him and two waited outside, according to Harry," Ed Sitwell said.

"I'll be in touch," Fargo said. "I want to talk to Anderson."

"We're coming along," Carl Weathers said as they began to follow him, to the low-roofed house in front of the silver mine. Harry Anderson stepped outside as Fargo dismounted.

"I heard. I'm sorry," Fargo said.

"I never had a chance, couldn't even shoot one of the three that broke in here," Anderson said.

"Three? Mullins said four."

"Frank Mullins exaggerates everything. I ought to know. I was there," Anderson said as the others came up to form a half circle as they listened. "You fooled them with that shipment of rocks. A lot of good that did. They came here and cleaned me out. I should've shipped my silver later that day."

Fargo swore silently. The attack had been a new wrinkle and had clearly been an answer to his tricking them. They could have waited to strike at the next shipment, but they had chosen to hit back. It had been more than an attack. It had been a gesture. Somebody had refused to be cheated. Fargo's eyes narrowed as the thought stayed in his mind. It was important, he felt certain, though he couldn't define why.

"Nothing you've done has helped one damn bit, Fargo," Ed Sitwell said. "You haven't been able to track them anywhere."

"So far as we're concerned, you're through, Fargo," Clay Sanborn put in, triumphant malice in his voice.

"That's up to Sam Bradbury. He hired me," Fargo said.

"Then we'll see he fires you. It'll be his last official act before we vote him out," Sanborn said.

"You think getting rid of Sam Bradbury is going to stop these attacks?" Fargo questioned.

"We don't say that, but we'll get a Mayor with better ideas on how to stop them, such as maybe calling in the army," Tom Maxwell said.

"The army won't help you one damn bit. They're too busy and this isn't army business," Fargo said and laughed. "But as of now I'm still hired. You all know a man named Tim Halligan. Where might I find him?"

"Tim Halligan?" Luke Willis frowned. "You think he's part of this?"

"I'm sure of it," Fargo said.

The men exchanged skeptical glances but Sitwell spoke up. "He was hanging out in Rockside, that's some five miles south," Sitwell said. "Some of my men saw him there one day. Maybe Karen Bradbury can tell you more. She was the last one he worked for around here."

"I asked her. She didn't know anything about him," Fargo said as he climbed onto the Ovaro. "I'll go have a look in Rockside."

"We'll be having a talk with the mayor," Clay Sanborn said.

"Be my guest," Fargo said as he put the horse into a canter. He didn't really blame them, he mused as he rode on. They were hurting bad, frustrated and afraid and so far he hadn't been able to come up with any answers. Maybe he would this time; he frowned as he rode on, skirted town, and stopped at Barnaby's shack. Barnaby grimaced when he finished telling him what had happened.

"They're fools wanting to fire you," the old-timer said. "You're the only chance they have to get at the bottom of this."

"They're too angry for straight thinking. I stopped by because I'm going to need your help. I may be in Rockside a few days. I want you to watch Clay Sanborn. Harry Anderson's hurting. I want to know if Sanborn contacts him. But stay hidden. I don't want him spotting you."

"He won't," Barnaby said. "I've trailed too many bobcats to be spotted by a weasel like that."

"I'll see you when I get back," Fargo said and turned the Ovaro south. He rode slowly, letting thoughts revolve in his mind, examining every little detail he knew so far and had to admit it wasn't a great deal. But there were some things that were beginning to paint a picture, lines still not connected but drawing closer. He continued his musings until he reached the town of Rockside as the day began to draw to a close. Rockside was a far cry from Windsor Bell, a grubby little place made up mostly of storage sheds and run-down wagon shops, the saloon the largest structure in the town. The wagons parked along the main street were mostly worn one-horse utility rigs, a few marked with Wheeler Wagon Company nameplates and others carrying Owensboro trademarks. Most of the men he saw on the street looked like drifters and cowhands who'd seen better days. It was, he decided, a perfect spot for Tim Halligan to recruit his thieves.

Fargo halted before the saloon, dropped the Ovaro's reins across the hitching bar and stepped into a wide room that fitted the rest of Rockside, mostly a weather-beaten bar, sawdust covering the floor, three worn girls seated at a round table, and a dozen men at the bar. The bartender, a portly man wearing a stained white shirt, greeted Fargo with a mechanical smile. "A little bourbon and a little information," Fargo said with a smile.

"I can give you the first. Don't know about the second." The man smiled back.

Fargo took a sip of the bourbon poured for him. Poor quality slop, he commented silently while he smiled and made it appear as if he were used to that kind of whiskey. "I'm looking for work," he said. "I'm not too particular what it is. I hear a man named Tim Halligen is hiring."

"Where'd you hear that?" the bartender asked cautiously.

"Here and there. Word gets around," Fargo said casually. "Thought maybe you could tell me where I can find Halligan."

"Nobody finds Tim Halligan. But he might come to see you," the bartender said. "I might be able to get word to him."

Fargo removed a five-dollar bill from his pocket and

folded it under his glass. "I'd appreciate that," he said.

"Stop by at noon tomorrow. No promises, though," the bartender said.

"Naturally." Fargo smiled. "See you at noon." He left the remainder of the drink and strolled from the saloon, took the Ovaro and walked the horse across the street to the blackness alongside a wide storage structure. He pushed the horse deeper into the shadows as he dropped to one knee and watched the saloon doors. His guess had been right. Halligan had to have some practical means to make his contacts and hire his men. The saloon was the logical focal point for such contacts. As he watched, four men sauntered in and out of the saloon, then another, when suddenly a sixth one appeared. No sauntering with this one as he hurried purposefully to his horse, pulled himself into the saddle, and set out at a fast canter.

Fargo smiled, let him almost reach the end of town before he followed after him. The man rode along a narrow path and Fargo hung back, stayed against a row of sycamore as the man climbed a low hill and followed an overgrown trail that ended at a small clearing surrounded by dense tree cover. A hut occupied the center of the clearing, a light burning brightly inside and the door opened as the rider came to a halt. A man stepped out, tall and thin-framed, a rifle in his hands. Fargo had halted too far away to see anything else about the man who was for the most part silhouetted in the light from the doorway. He stepped back into the hut and the visitor went with him.

Fargo slid from the saddle and led the pinto through the trees that surrounded the hut. He halted as close as he dared to come and sank down on one knee to wait. The wait was a short one as the visitor emerged a few minutes later, climbed onto his horse, and rode away. Fargo waited till the sound of the hoofbeats faded and then stepped from the trees, crossed the small open space, and knocked at the door of the hut. "Now what?" he heard Halligan say with irritation as he yanked the door open, halted, and stared. Fargo made no move to his Colt and the man drew his gun instantly. "Who're you, Mister?" Halligan growled.

"I'm the one looking for work, the one you just heard about," Fargo said blandly and saw the frown of surprise come into the man's face. Tim Halligan fit his description, his face sharp and tight, a meanness to the mouth.

"How the hell did you find me?" Halligan asked.

"It wasn't hard. I just followed that errand boy." Fargo smiled.

Halligan's eyes narrowed. "Smart," he grunted. "Smarter than the kind I usually hire, I'll give you that. Come in." He stepped back into the hut and Fargo entered, saw a single room so cluttered with boxes and crates that it was impossible to tell if Halligan had any loot there from the robberies. "How'd you get my name?" Halligan said, dropping his gun back into its holster.

"One of your men was killed during a raid. I happened to be near. He was still alive when I reached him. He told me your name, said to tell you he'd been shot," Fargo said. "He packed it in a few minutes later and I came looking."

Tim Halligan's eyes shrewdly examined the big man in front of him. "You don't look like you need work," he observed.

Fargo let nonchalance act as a mask. "I make it a point not to look like the average saddle tramp," he said.

"You know what the hands I hire do?" Halligan asked.

"No, but I can ride and I can shoot. I figure that ought to cover most things," Fargo said, keeping an easy confidence.

Halligan studied him another long moment. "You've got a way with you. Maybe you could fit in," he said. "What's your name?"

"O'Graf," Fargo said.

"Funny sort of name," Halligan said.

"My folks were Irish and German," Fargo said.

Halligan's lips pursed. "I'd like the rest of my men to meet you. I want men who work together well. If they go along I'll use you," he said. "Come back here at four tomorrow afternoon."

"Fair enough," Fargo said and Halligan watched him climb onto the Ovaro. The man watched him ride off without returning his wave. But Fargo smiled as he rode into the night. It had gone well. The answer he wanted would come once he was accepted. He rode into a low hill, found a spot under a pair of red ashes and bedded down and let himself sleep late into the morning. He found a stream and washed leisurely, relaxed, stayed away from Rockside and Halligan's hut until the sun began to slide down the sky.

He rode down to Halligan's hut and saw the small knot of men with Halligan, their horses to one side. He felt confident. The only members of Halligan's crew that might have been able to identify him could no longer identify anyone. He halted, swung from the saddle as the others turned to him and Halligan stepped forward. The man smiled, a sharp, wolfish smile. "This here is Mr. O'Graf, boys," he said. "Step up and shake his hand." Two of the men came forward, hands extended, when both suddenly spun and Fargo felt his arms seized. A third man ran behind him to help hold his arms back. He started to protest when he saw Halligan swinging his gun butt in a quick arc. Fargo felt the blow crash against the side of his temple and the world went gray as he sank to his knees.

He shook his head and the grayness lifted and he saw he was facedown on the ground. "Bastard," Halligan said and Fargo grunted in pain as the kick landed in his side. He was yanked to his feet and saw that Halligan already had his Colt stuffed into his belt. "Tie his hands," Halligan ordered. "In front of him so's he can hold his saddle horn." Two of the men wrapped a length of rope that bound his wrists together as Halligan snarled at him. "Goddamn smartass. You almost got away with it," the man said.

"Nothing ventured, nothing gained," Fargo said and received a blow to his belly that doubled him up.

"Don't sass me, bastard," Halligan said.

"What do we do with him, boss?" one of the others asked.

"I was told to take him into Indiana, a day or two away and lose him there," Halligan said.

"Kill him there?" the man queried.

"No, just dump him so it'll take him a few days to get back," Halligan said. "But I'm not wastin' all that time on him. But I don't want him found here, either. Four of you take him up to the cliffs. Kill him and throw him into the ravine."

"It's done," one of the men said and Fargo was hoisted onto the Ovaro. One of the men rode in front of him, one flanked him on each side, and the fourth rode behind. They shepherded him away, climbed a rise and traveled along a flat stretch until the granite cliffs rose up in the distance. Fargo's thoughts raced. He had one answer. Halligan wasn't on his own. He worked for someone and Fargo uttered a wry oath to himself. He had asked about Halligan of everyone. Somebody decided he might track the man down and decided a fast trip to Halligan was necessary. That somebody was getting to seem more and more like Clay Sanborn. But he'd never know if that was right unless he could find a way to save his neck, Fargo realized as the horses began to climb a path up into the cliffs.

The land was thick with rocks and a few scraggly red mulberry clinging to the barren soil. The first ravine came into sight on his left, a dry, rock-strewn drop followed by another with steeper sides. The riding room narrowed as they bordered the ravine and Fargo swore silently. There was no way he could reach the throwing knife in its calf holster, even if his hands were untied, and his eyes went down into the ravine again. The sides sloped, loose rock clinging to them and the bottom rocks had grown smaller. He saw where a river had coursed through the bottom at one time, a swath relatively free of stones. The desperate plan took instant shape in his thoughts. The day was fading. They wouldn't wait much longer. He turned the chances over again in his mind.

It might take getting shot, he grimaced. But getting shot was better than getting killed and that was his only alternative. His eyes scanned the two men alongside him. They were riding casually. He had already sized up the man who rode behind, an ordinary hand with gnarled fingers. He wouldn't be a fast draw. Fargo's eyes went down into the ravine again. He might avoid being killed but he sure couldn't avoid being bruised. He drew a deep breath, gathered the powerful muscles of his calves and thighs, slowly half-rose in the saddle and flung himself sideways. He slammed into the rider on his right and the man flew sideways off his horse, Fargo going with him.

133

But Fargo was prepared, managed to land on his feet as the other man hit the rocky ground on his back. Fargo, his hands still tied behind him, dived over the edge of the ravine, head first, swung his body around as he began to roll. He heard his own grunt of pain as he slammed into rocks, felt the tearing at his flesh as sharp-edged stones dug into him. The shots erupted then, kicking up stones inches from him as he rolled downward and the pain consumed his body. The shots and the stones became one and he wasn't sure if the terrible, sharp pain was caused by bullets or rocks. They were still firing, and they weren't good shots or he'd be dead, he realized dimly and then suddenly he was landing hard onto the bottom of the ravine, the flattened path where the river had once run. He lay still, facedown, and two more shots kicked up stones near his face. He forced himself to continue to remain motionless and the shots ended.

It was almost dark and a long way down into the ravine. He had counted on their not climbing down after him and he'd been right. He didn't know when they left but no one climbed down. They decided the motionless form was dead and rode away and he was left in the dark. He lay still, not playing 'possum any longer but simply battered and bruised and too exhausted to move. His eyes closed, he half slept, let strength slowly ebb back to him. The moon was high when he pulled his eyes open, the ravine silent as a tomb. He moved and cried out, every part of his body still burning with pain. But fighting down waves of nausea, he drew his legs up and, maneuvering his bound hands, he pulled the razor-sharp, double-edged throwing knife from its calf holster.

Cursing at the pain that continued to assault him, he turned the knife in his fingers until he brought the edge against his wrist ropes. He began little sawing motions, able to move the knife but a half inch each way. He had to stop every few minutes as his fingers cramped, wait for them to unstiffen and then begin again. It was a slow and laborious process and each period he could saw grew shorter as his fingers cramped more quickly. Yet he stayed at it and gritted his teeth against the burning pain of his body, and his forehead was coated with perspiration as the moon began to slide down to the far end of the blue-black sky. He had just begun the sawing motion again after letting his fingers unstiffen when, so suddenly that he fell backward, the ropes gave way and parted.

He lay on his back for a few minutes and then pushed to a seated position and began to examine himself. Two bullets had hit him, luckily both passing clean through nonvital areas, one through the back of his thigh, the other through the skin at the right side of his waist. The rest of the cuts and welts on his body came from the stones and rocks he'd hit as he rolled down the side of the ravine. He turned, unwilling to try standing up yet, and began to crawl up the side of the ravine. He paused often to rest his weakened body and draw in deep drafts of air, but the top of the ravine finally appeared and he pulled himself over the edge and lay flat on the ground.

He gave a low whistle, waited and hoped, and finally heard the sound of the Ovaro moving toward him. Pushing to his feet, Fargo swayed a moment as waves of dizziness swept through him and he realized how weakened he was. The blood from all his wounds and bruises had stopped flowing and congealed on his skin as a sticky, uncomfortable ooze and he winced as he pulled himself onto the horse. He sat in the saddle, not moving for a long moment as he fought away another wave of dizziness. The moon had moved down toward the horizon, he saw. The morning sun would be up in a few hours and he began to walk the Ovaro downward along the rock-limned cliffsides. The four men had reported that they'd killed him, he was certain of that. That meant Halligan was feeling secure. But he wasn't ready for Halligan yet, Fargo knew. His body needed to restore itself. Yet he hadn't the luxury of time, he realized.

If most of the others collapsed financially, the game could be over. Tim Halligan would be paid off and sent on his way and there'd be only suspicions, perhaps not even that, left. And one big winner. Fargo swore softly as the Ovaro continued down the rocky passage. Tim Halligan was still the key to that final answer he wanted. Fargo frowned as he finally reached the bottom of the stone cliffs. The first hint of the new day was beginning to streak the sky over the hills and Fargo turned the pinto to the stream he had found yesterday. When he reached it, the sun had come up to bathe the land with its warmth. He halted, slid from the horse and shed clothes and immersed his body in the waters of the stream. He felt the congealed blood slowly wash away as he lay back and closed his eyes.

He stayed lying in the stream for most of the morning, letting the cooling water soothe the burning still in his body. When he finally stepped from the stream he used a roll of bandages from his saddlebag to wrap the two places where the bullets had passed through him and which were still seeping blood. He stretched out on the grass then, naked, his gunbelt beside him, and let the sun's healing warmth penetrate his body. His own strength and recuperative power began to assert itself under the sun's wonderful restorative force and he added the power of sleep. When he woke, the day was nearing an end but he felt the strength in his body, not all returned by any means, but enough for him to go on. He dressed and climbed onto the Ovaro and began his way back to Tim Halligan's cabin. The day had turned into night before he reached it and when he pushed through the circle of trees he halted, and the soft oath hissed from his lips as he saw the six horses outside.

He could hear the voices from within the hut and he slid from the horse, drew the throwing knife from its calf holster, and hurried across the small clearing at a crouch. He paused near the cabin, eyed the partially open door, and decided on the lone window. He crept to the spot and carefully raised his head enough to let him peer inside. Halligan was paying each of the others with a wad of bills and small bags of silver, their voices clear enough through the window. "Good luck to you," Halligan said. "I told you it'd be worthwhile."

"You sure did, boss," one of the others said.

"You going to stick around here now?" another asked as he shoved the money into his pocket.

"No, I'll be moving on, maybe down Texas way," Halligan said. "I'll probably pack and be started tomorrow."

"Maybe we'll meet up again," another said.

"Maybe." Halligan nodded as he paid the last of the six.

Fargo dropped low and ran from the window in a crouch before the men started to come out. He disappeared into the trees, dropped to one knee and watched as the six men left the cabin, climbed onto the horses and rode away. Halligan pulled the door almost closed, leaving it six inches ajar and Fargo frowned into the darkness. Something was wrong. It was all coming to an end too soon. Even with the raid that took all Harry Anderson's silver, they couldn't have all collapsed that quickly. They were going to have him fired and vote out Sam Bradbury. But there was no talk of anything else.

Fargo's frown continued to crease his brow. He'd been certain it would take at least one more robbery, maybe two, to bring them all down. Yet here it was all ending, the final payment made. It just didn't add up. It was too soon. He stared at the hut. The answer was inside and once again he left the trees in a crouch, the knife in his hand. He knew he could just wait for a chance to send the blade hurtling into Halligan. That would be the safest course, but it wouldn't give him any answers. Even if he brought Halligan down by sinking the blade into his leg the man would have time to draw and fire. He'd have to charge Halligan by surprise, Fargo realized, get to him before he could react.

It wouldn't be easy, Fargo muttered as he reached the door of the hut. He heard Halligan inside, tossing around boxes and Fargo slid against the outer wall of the hut, not more than a foot from the door. His back pressed against the hut, he sank down and scooped up a handful of small stones, rose and tossed half of them against the base of the door. He heard Halligan grow silent inside the cabin and he tossed the other half of the stones against the door. Halligan's footsteps sounded and Fargo stayed flattened against the wall of the hut as the door opened and Halligan stepped out, the six-gun in his hand.

Fargo allowed him only a split second to peer into the darkness before striking, his hand coming around in an arc, sinking the blade into Halligan's wrist. "Ow, Jesus," Halligan screamed and the gun fell from his hand. He yanked his arm away, half turned to see Fargo pulling the knife back and Fargo saw the surprise in his face. Fargo rushed forward, jabbed the knife tip under Halligan's jaw as the man took a half step backward.

"One wrong move and I'll ram it through your head," Fargo said.

Halligan's eyes were small circles of fury. "Those sonofabitches. They lied to me," he said.

"They made a mistake," Fargo said. He took the blade from under Halligan's jaw as he stepped back, bent down to pick up the six-gun. He realized he'd misjudged the quickness of the man as Halligan's kick shot out, glanced off his arm and against his chest as he was picking up the gun. Fargo fell back off-balance, but he kept his hand on the gun and started to bring the weapon up when Halligan dived through the open door and into the cabin. He kicked the door shut with his foot as Fargo shot low but missed and the bullet slammed into the door.

Fargo rose, the gun in his hand as he dropped the knife into his pocket. He charged forward, lowered his shoulder, and hurtled into the door. It flew open and he roared into the hut to see Halligan with the shotgun raised. "Shit," Fargo swore as he dived to the floor and felt the shotgun blast singe his hair. Facedown on the floor, he started to rise and saw Halligan smash down at him with the stock of the gun. He got one arm up, partly deflected the blow but still took most of it against the side of his head. A wave of pain shot through him and he glimpsed Halligan's leg as the man stepped in to smash the gun stock down at him again.

Fargo curled his arm around the man's ankle and pulled and heard Halligan's grunt as he went down and his blow went wild. Fargo found the half-second to bring a punch up from the floor that landed in Halligan's belly and the man grunted and fell back. Fargo's glance swept the floor, spied the six-gun where it had skidded some three feet away and he rolled, dived for it only to feel Halligan land atop him. The man got one arm around his neck, pulled hard and Fargo felt his breath cut off instantly. But Halligan hadn't landed squarely on him and Fargo managed to dig one foot into the earthen floor of the hut, lift and push the man's body enough for him to loosen his throat grip. The moment of respite was all he needed and Fargo tore away from Halligan's arm, rolled and kicked out and his blow caught his foe in the chest. Halligan fell sideways but the shotgun was only inches from him and he seized it with both hands, spun to his feet, and charged forward with the gun, using the stock again as a club.

Fargo saw that the six-gun was too far to reach without being clubbed and he rolled, avoided Halligan's blow, landed on his back, and shot out both legs as Halligan came at him again. The double kick caught Halligan in his side as the man managed to twist his body. The kick had enough power in it to send Halligan falling sideways but, with an oath, Fargo saw him hit the floor only inches from the six-gun. Halligan's hand was closing around the gun as Fargo yanked the knife from his pocket. He had no time to aim carefully, only a split-second to throw as Halligan brought the gun up. The thin blade whistled through the air and Fargo swore as he saw it go through Halligan's neck. The man's finger automatically tightened on the trigger as he fell back, the shot going into the wall. Fargo rose, saw him drop the gun and reach up and pull the blade from his neck.

He held it in his hand for a moment, stared at it before he sank to his knees and slowly fell forward onto his face. His hand opened and the knife rolled out onto the floor as Fargo stepped to Halligan's quivering form. The thin stream of blood from the man's neck seemed harmless, but Fargo knew the vital arteries had been severed. He turned Halligan over and saw the man's face was already ashen. "Who hired you, dammit?" Fargo asked. Halligan's lips twitched, his body stiffened and then he went limp and Fargo heard the last breath hiss from his lips.

Fargo rose, grimaced, retrieved the knife, and then began to search through the clutter inside the hut. He found the money Halligan had kept for himself and he found the Colt Halligan had taken from him. But there was nothing else and Fargo walked from the hut. He brought the Ovaro out of the trees, swung onto the horse and rode slowly away, his brow wearing a deep furrow. Halligan would give no answers, yet perhaps, in an oblique way, he had. Fargo's frown stayed as he turned the horse north toward Windsor Bell.

8

The battle with Halligan had been more than he'd
expected and he hadn't had all his strength back yet.
He felt the fatigue pull at him as he rode and he
turned, found a spot beneath a sycamore and bedded
down. He slept heavily and made use of his inner
alarm clock to wake before dawn. The new morning
rose as he rode north and he reached Barnaby's shack
soon after to find Barnaby still toweling himself dry.
"God, Fargo, I was getting worried about you," Barnaby said.

"You had reason," Fargo said. "Tell me about
Sanborn first."

"You guessed right. He paid a visit to Harry Anderson the next day. I tailed him and watched. When he
left he stuffed a piece of paper into his pocket and
looked real pleased with himself," Barnaby said.

"A deed from Anderson for a loan, most likely."

"That keeps him number one, I'd say." Barnaby
frowned.

"Maybe," Fargo grunted.

"Maybe?" Barnaby echoed.

"I've no answer yet but I've been doing a lot of
thinking. I may have been barking up the wrong tree
in more ways than one," Fargo said.

"You want to explain that?" Barnaby said.

"Finish dressing and we ride, into the high hills
again," Fargo said.

"Be right with you." Barnaby nodded and hurried into the shack. He emerged, fully dressed, saddled the gray mare and fell in beside Fargo. "You want to tell me about it?" he asked as they rode.

"I think I've maybe been looking for trails that weren't there," Fargo said.

"You mean the tracks that just disappeared?" Barnaby said.

"Tracks don't disappear. Horses and riders don't vanish into thin air. They didn't exist," Fargo said. "I'll show you when we get there." He put the Ovaro into a canter and Barnaby stayed a few paces behind as Fargo circled around Windsor Bell, crossed in front of the plateau, and climbed into the high hills. He rode deep into the hills, upward to the high sheer wall of dirt and stone where Halligan's bandits had dropped their loot and doubled back on their tracks. Fargo halted and dismounted as he pointed to the hoofprints still clear in the ground. "They rode back and forth here, covering their tracks while they dropped the loot. Then they rode down out of the hills. I know that. I followed them twice," Fargo said.

"You came back here again but you couldn't find the prints of anyone picking up the bags. They just disappeared."

"Because there were no hoofprints to find," Fargo said and Barnaby stared at him. "Whoever picked up the loot was on foot. Whoever it was stepped into the hoofprints so there were no footprints to see. The damn missing prints led me straying too. I kept looking for caves large enough to hold horse and rider but there was no horse and no rider." Fargo stepped to the tall expanse of rock, dirt, and brush. He began to move his hands along the rock, stepping along the base of the towering cliffside, pressing into tall sections of mountain brush. Barnaby moved along with him, keeping back, and suddenly Fargo halted. "Over here," he called and Barnaby hurried forward.

"I'll be damned," Barnaby murmured as Fargo held back part of the brush that hid a narrow cleft in the rock, barely wide enough for a man to walk through.

"Let's go exploring," Fargo said as he stepped into the cleft in the rock and Barnaby followed. The cleft turned, snaked its way between the towering rocks, stayed narrow as Fargo's shoulders rubbed against both sides. At one point he had to turn his body sideways to fit through as the passageway narrowed. It returned to its former width and he glanced back to see Barnaby just behind him. "It's going downhill," Fargo called as the passage sloped and continued to slope. The cleft ran longer and deeper than he'd expected but it finally began to widen and Barnaby came up to walk alongside him. The passage moved farther downhill and suddenly widened again and scrub trees appeared to line the walls.

The stone walls curved away from each other and the rock footing became dirt-covered. "We're pretty near the end of it," Fargo said and stopped where a long branch extended from a scrubby tree. He motioned to the ground where hoofprints were imprinted in an aimless pattern. "The horse was tied here," Fargo said. "The bags were brought down through the cleft in the rocks to where the horse waited." Barnaby nodded and followed him as he pushed through a thin line of white ash where the hoofprints led. The land opened up, and below, at the bottom of a gentle slope, lay the valley and Ben Slocum's house in a direct line.

He glanced at Barnaby and saw the wry smile on the older man's mouth. "Guess this puts Ben and the valley folks right back next to Sanborn," Barnaby said, a long sigh accompanying his words.

"Could be." Fargo nodded.

"What about some Robin Hood? Was that a song and dance they gave us about the bags being left for them?"

"I don't think so. We saw Slocum go out and pull the bag out of the geraniums," Fargo said.

"That we did," Barnaby agreed. "Then what's it all mean?"

Fargo turned and started back the way they had come through the narrow cleft. "I'm not sure yet. I've got to do some more putting together," he said as he climbed along the crevice to emerge where the Ovaro and the gray mare waited. "But first I'll stop at Sam Bradbury's," Fargo said.

"I'll be at the shack," Barnaby said and followed Fargo down from the high hills to leave him as the town came into sight. Fargo walked the horse into Windsor Bell and he had just reached the mayor's house when he saw Libby carrying two bulging traveling bags. She wore a yellow traveling suit with a bustle at the rear and her eyes shot angry defiance at him as he reined to a halt.

"Where are you going?" he asked.

"To the stage," she snapped.

"Where's the mayor?" Fargo questioned.

"Inside, only he's not the mayor anymore. They threw him out," Libby said.

"And you're leaving him," Fargo said.

"Damn right," Libby said coldly.

"I knew you were hardly the faithful wife but I thought you'd stick around long enough to give him a little support. My mistake," Fargo said.

"That's right; your mistake. As the wife of the mayor I had some clout in this town. They never liked me but they had to be nice to me. I'm not staying around as the wife of a nobody," Libby said.

"He knew he was close to being removed. I'm sure this hit at him a lot harder," Fargo said.

"You know, I think he expected this as much as he did getting thrown out," she said. "He didn't seem at all surprised. He just looked sad."

"I was going to give him my condolences. I think I'll congratulate him," Fargo said.

"Go to hell," Libby hissed and stalked off with her bags.

Fargo watched her go for a moment and then went into the house to find Sam Bradbury at his desk, a bottle of whiskey in front of him. The man looked up at him and Fargo saw his eyes were indeed filled with a resigned sadness. "Just met Libby," Fargo said.

"Then you know," Bradbury said and Fargo nodded. "They told me to fire you as my last official act but you'd disappeared so they voted me out anyway. They said that'd take care of you too."

"Guess it does," Fargo agreed.

"I thought you'd seen the writing on the wall and taken off," Bradbury said.

"Wrong," Fargo said.

"You come back with the answer?" the man asked.

"Maybe soon," Fargo said. "I think I'm getting close."

Bradbury shrugged as he reached for the bottle. "It's not your concern anymore, Fargo. Forget it and go your way," he said.

"Can't do that," Fargo said. "You hired me to do a job. I'm going to see it through."

"Principles, eh?"

"Guess so. On some things, anyway."

"Too bad Libby didn't have more," the man said and Fargo shot him a sharp glance.

"Meaning what exactly?" he asked cautiously.

"Walking out on me like this," Sam Bradbury said,

hurt and indignation coming into his face. "But then Karen said I'd be happier without her."

"How'd Karen hear Libby was leaving you?" Fargo asked.

"Libby told me she was leaving two days ago, when they voted me out as mayor. Karen stopped by that night and I told her," Bradbury said and took a drink from the bottle. "I know Karen always hated Libby and maybe she was right."

"I'll be in touch, soon as I'm sure," Fargo said and left Sam Bradbury taking another drink from the bottle. The main street of town was bustling and crowded as he walked the Ovaro past the saloon and paused when he came upon Tom Maxwell in a buckboard. "Find a new mayor yet?" he asked.

"Not yet but Carl Weathers brought a payroll to the bank without being attacked," the man said. "Sort of made us all start wonderin' about Sam Bradbury."

"And me, too, I suppose," Fargo said.

There was admission in the man's half shrug. "Clay Sanborn wondered if maybe Sam hired you so he'd be sure you didn't find out anything."

"Is that so?" Fargo said blandly. "Tell Clay Sanborn he's all wrong. Tell him I've found out a lot."

Tom Maxwell's brows lifted. "You have? I'm sure we'd all like to know what."

"When the time comes," Fargo said, and tossed Maxwell an enigmatic smile as he moved the horse on. He heard Maxwell put the buckboard into a dirt-throwing start as he rushed away. Fargo reined to a halt only a street farther on when he saw Ben Slocum and two men lifting a new plow into an old wagon. "Get yourselves another gift?" Fargo speared. "New plows are expensive. Silver this time, was it?"

"None of your damn business," Ben Slocum said. "You were fired, we heard."

"You heard right," Fargo said.

"Then be on your way," Slocum growled.

"In time. I'm just naturally curious," Fargo said.

"That can get you naturally dead," the man muttered.

"Or satisfied," Fargo said and spurred the Ovaro on. He took the path into the low hills and the small pond where he dismounted and stretched out in the sun. As the day went by, he sifted through everything he had learned, piece by piece, bit by bit, person by person. He went over details, again and again, sorting, rejecting, fitting together the likely and the unlikely and the day became night before he finished. He took to the saddle and rode with the grimness of finality an invisible but heavy cloak and reached Barnaby's shack. "You've been a real help, old-timer," he said. "Got one last chore for you."

"I'm listening," Barnaby said.

"Spread the word tomorrow. Tell them all I have the answer. I know who's been behind it all. Tell Ben Slocum and tell the rich men on the plateau. I don't expect you'll have to tell everyone. Word will spread damn fast."

"You can count on it," Barnaby said.

"Tell them one thing more. Tell them I'll be waiting where the bags were dropped, midnight tomorrow. The right one can give up to me there. It'll be easier that way."

"And if nobody shows?" Barnaby asked.

"I'll come gunning. I don't want to do that but I will and that won't end as nice," Fargo said.

"You sure about all this?" Barnaby frowned.

"I'm sure," Fargo said.

"But you're not telling me," the older man said.

"I'm not getting anyone else involved now. You'll be just the messenger. That way nobody will get any ideas about hitting back at you. People get desperate at showdown time," Fargo said and Barnaby nodded gravely and Fargo saw his eyes studying him.

"You don't look like a man who's just won," Barnaby commented.

"Sometimes there's not as much satisfaction in winning as there should be," Fargo said. "Thanks again, Barnaby."

He rode quickly away, unwilling to be the target of the old man's sagacity. Returning to the low hills, he found a comfortable spot to bed down, chewed on a stick of cold beef jerky, and finally stretched out to sleep. He took a while to find slumber, his thoughts filled with the less than appealing aspects of the human condition. They danced through his mind like so many ghouls at a funeral, hate, greed, deceit, revenge, all those things that could so easily twist decency, honor, loyalty, even love, out of shape. But he finally pushed away dark thoughts and forced himself to find sleep until the morning sun woke him.

He rose, breakfasted on tasty, deep gold-yellow Grimes Goldens—apples he didn't often get to enjoy— and he took his leisure with the fruit and the morning. He stayed deep in the hills until the day finally came to a close when he slowly made his way across the low hill country and up into the ruggedness of the high hills. He timed his arrival at the spot to reach there a half hour before the moon hung in the midnight sky and he tethered the Ovaro deep in the trees across from the opening of the rock cleft. He moved closer to the brush that covered the cleft but stayed inside the trees, leaned back on a convenient trunk, and listened to the night sounds.

The moon had begun to move away from its midnight high when he caught the faint sound. It came from the tall rock formation where the ragged brush hid the narrow cleft, a sound most listeners would not have picked up. He waited, heard it again, the thick scrub brush being carefully pushed aside and then silence again. His visitor was waiting, being very careful. Just as he was; he smiled. He stepped to the edge of the trees, then into the open, a calculated risk, yet less of one than many he'd taken in his lifetime. There'd be no instant blast of gunfire from out of the darkness. Curiosity was one of the most powerful forces of human nature. It had to be satisfied. He counted on that. Still, he kept his hand on the butt of the Colt at his side.

"Come on out, Karen," he said softly.

The dry, scraggly brush parted and the slender shape stepped forward, a Spencer repeater rifle in her hands. The light blue eyes flamed with the blue fire he had seen at another time and another place. Passion and fury were indeed handmaidens. "Damn you, Fargo. How did you know?" she said.

"I didn't, not for a long while," he said. "I even had a few last moments of doubt yesterday when I met Libby leaving. But then I thought it through, all the little things. The little things always count."

"Something put you onto it," she said.

"Tim Halligan," Fargo told her and saw the tiny furrow touch her smooth forehead. "He said his orders were to dump me alive somewhere in Indiana. I knew Clay Sanborn or Slocum would've told him to kill me. That meant his orders had come from somebody with a little compassion, or maybe just memories. The price of sentiment, honey."

Her smile was wry. "How true," she murmured.

"The rest began to come then, like that night you finally told me to come visit. You made sure I wouldn't be out roaming that night. I might have come onto the Anderson attack. But I didn't make the connection then."

"What made you make it?" Karen questioned.

"That night and the rocks," he said and she frowned. "They suddenly fitted."

"How?"

"You refused to be refused, remember?" The wryness was in her smile again. "The attack was ordered by someone who refused to be tricked, someone who had to get their way."

"Very good," she said.

"You got to Halligan to warn him. But anyone could've done that. Even though I began to think about you, I couldn't find a motive. Then you gave it to me," Fargo said and her eyes questioned again. "I watched Halligan pay off his men. It was over, ended, and I wondered why. I couldn't figure that until I came back and learned Libby was leaving your father. I had the motive then. It was all to make her leave. You knew that if he was no longer mayor she'd walk out on him. Your hate for her did it."

"She was rotten. He couldn't see it but I knew. I had to help him. I love my father," Karen said.

"No, that love became an obsession. An obsession twists love out of shape, turns it into something ugly," he said.

"No," she said, her voice rising. "I had to get rid of her. It was the right thing to do."

"Sorry, honey. No sale," Fargo said.

"Dammit, I did it because I love my father."

"Because you've an obsession," he said doggedly.

"I didn't do it for the money. I left part of it for the valley folks every time," she said, defensive anger coming into her voice.

"Not out of the goodness of your heart. You knew they'd be so happy they'd take the money and start buying things. You knew they'd point the finger at themselves. You set them up. Don't give me any hearts and flowers on that one, honey," he said and her eyes narrowed.

"Now what?" she said and he slid a half step closer to her. She wasn't gripping the rifle as tightly as she had when she stepped from the rocks.

"You know what?" he said quietly.

"You wouldn't. You couldn't. You've forgotten that night already? I can't believe that," she said.

"I haven't forgotten. Doesn't change things though," he said and slid another step closer.

"Yes, it does. It has to," she said, no pleading in her voice, just a certainty. "It can't be any other way. I did what was right."

He peered at her, into the light blue eyes and he suddenly felt a terrible sadness. She believed in what she said, believed wholly and completely. Obsessions allowed for no doubts. She was searching his face, her hands on the gun still relaxed. It was now or perhaps never, he knew. Obsessions allowed for no retreats, either. His arm shot out, one hand closing around the barrel of the rifle as he twisted. Her finger tightened and the shot hurled into the air and he heard the bullet smash into a stone. He twisted harder and the rifle tore from her grip and he stepped back, dodged her wild swing and caught her arm. "Stop it," he said, held her until he felt her relax, then stepped back.

"You can't take me in, Fargo. You understand. I know you understand," she said.

"Yes," he said and nodded. "I understand something else, too. A lot of innocent men were killed because of your little scheme—ranch hands riding guard, employees, ordinary men carrying out their boss's orders. You hired gunhands who killed and robbed, all so your Pa would be thrown out of office and Libby would leave him. There was nothing right or good about any of it, honey. There was only you and your obsession."

He was surprised by the real hurt he saw in her eyes. "I didn't expect you'd be like this, Fargo," she said.

"I didn't exactly expect you'd turn out this way either," he said.

"I could have given Tim Halligan orders to kill you," she reminded him.

"As I said, the price of sentiment," he answered. "The innocent men killed because of what you schemed up to satisfy your obsession deserve justice."

The voice cut in from the trees. "It's an unjust world, Fargo. This will be one more injustice," it said and Fargo saw Sam Bradbury step from the brush against the rocks. He carried a Colt Patterson aimed to fire. "Put the rifle down," the man said.

Fargo eye'd the man's gun. It didn't waver and he knew he'd never be able to swing the rifle around to fire quickly enough to avoid a bullet from slamming into him. He opened his hands and the rifle dropped to the ground.

"Daddy," Karen's voice exploded. "How did you get here?"

"I waited outside your place and followed you when you left," Bradbury said.

"Goddamn, you knew all along?" Fargo frowned.

"No. I didn't know until Karen came to visit the other day," the man said, his glance going to his daughter, paternal tolerance in his eyes. "Remember how you smiled when I told you they'd voted me out?" he said. "It was all there in that smile—satisfaction, victory, triumph. I'd seen that smile before, since you were a little girl, every time you won something."

Fargo's eyes went to Karen and saw the smile come to her face, almost sheepish. "I told you I'd a room ready for you at my place," she said to her father. "I told you you had no reason to worry about anything."

"Yes," Sam Bradbury said. "But the words didn't really tell me anything. It was the smile."

Fargo felt a coldness gathering inside him. "I'm real touched by all this," he bit out. "But I'm taking her in."

"No, I can't let you," the man said. "It's as simple as that, Fargo. You promise to ride out of here and never come back and you can go. I know you're a man of your word."

"The others will be asking and wondering," Fargo said.

"They'll decide you were nothing but talk," Bradbury said. "You know that's exactly what will happen."

Fargo's glance went to Karen and then back to her father. She still had her obsession, now her victory, and he had nothing left but her. They'd cling to each other. Maybe they always had. But all those innocent men still deserved justice. He couldn't just walk away from that.

"I'll tell you what will happen," Fargo said. "You may put a bullet in me but not fast enough to stop me from getting one of you, maybe both of you. You were at the contest. You saw me draw and shoot."

Sam Bradbury surprised him by his calm. "Yes, I was there. I'm sure you can draw fast enough to do just that," the man said. "That's why I took some added precautions."

"Precautions?" Fargo frowned.

"Let's say added reasons to convince you to cooperate. I paid a visit to Barnaby. I know he's been a real help to you. Right now he's tied up in his shack. There's a stick of dynamite in there with him. It's on a long fuse that's been burning for the last hour and a half. It's got another half hour to burn, give or take a few minutes either way. Now, you can try to make it back there in a half hour or just let him blow up."

"You old bastard," Fargo growled.

"I told you it was an unjust world, Fargo. You're really quite fortunate. You can choose which injustice you want to live with. Most men never get a chance to do that," Sam Bradbury said. "Don't take too long to decide. I figure that fuse is burning an inch a minute."

Fargo felt the fury whirl inside him and with it, the helplessness. Enough innocent men had been killed. He couldn't add Barnaby to the list. He gave a low whistle and the Ovaro came out of the trees and he climbed onto the horse. "Don't start counting chickens," he flung back as he sent the Ovaro into a gallop. He cursed into the wind as he kept the horse going full out down the slopes, skirting trees, grateful for the moonlight that let him maintain speed. But he knew the unreliability of fuses. They could gather speed on their own. His frantic race through the night could be in vain.

He flung the thought from his mind and let Karen and Sam Bradbury fill his thoughts. He knew what they planned. They had at least five hours to ride through the night, five hours head start. He'd not be able to even hunt for their trail before daybreak. All in all, by the time he picked it up, they could have seven hours head start. They'd use Karen's fastest horses, of course. There was no certainty he'd ever be able to catch up to them, he realized, broke off further thoughts as the Ovaro reached the flat land and was able to increase speed.

He skirted the edge of the plateau and finally he was racing through the dark and deserted streets of town, the most direct path to Barnaby's shack. He was cursing and the Ovaro was breathing hard as he neared the shack and Fargo hoped against hope that the night would not shatter with sound. The shack came into view, still standing, the door open and the lamplight on inside. Fargo skidded the horse to a halt and leaped to the ground. He could see Barnaby inside the shack, bound in the big chair, and along the ground, snaking through the open door, he saw the charred line of the burned fuse. His lips pulled back as he saw the burning end of the fuse, less than an inch from the stick of dynamite at the edge of the chair. It was sparking, burning fast. There was no way he could cross the distance in time, he knew, and he drew the Colt as he dropped to the ground, took a split second to aim and fired. If he missed, he'd join Barnaby in being blown to bits, he knew.

He exploded in a shout as he saw the end of the rope go up in shreds as the bullet severed it and the burning fuse sputtered to a halt. There was perhaps a half inch of rope left tied to the stick of dynamite he saw and he pushed to his feet and stepped into the shack. Barnaby stared up at him, every crinkle in his face ashen. "That's cutting it a mite close, I'd say," Barnaby muttered.

"I'd go along with that," Fargo said as he carefully picked up the stick of dynamite and carried it outside. He returned and untied Barnaby.

"I'd also say you're a sight for sore eyes, but that wouldn't be the half of it. What the hell got into Sam Bradbury?" Barnaby asked.

"Pain and love, a lifetime of caring, the ties of a father for his daughter, pick any one you like. Blood's not just thicker than water. It's thicker than truth, sometimes," Fargo said and quickly told him the rest. He was back astride the Ovaro when he finished.

"I'd go with you but I know I'd only slow you

156

down," Barnaby said. "Think you'll catch up with them?"

"I'm damn sure going to try," Fargo bit out. "You've a new sheriff in town. Go to him. Lay it out for him. Tell him to expect me back."

Barnaby nodded as Fargo put the Ovaro into a fast canter, unwilling to push the horse any harder than he had to until it became necessary. He decided to save time and rode directly to Karen's place, certain they had to have stopped there. A man stood beside one of the corrals as he rode up, medium height and on the young side. He came forward as Fargo halted. "Looking for somebody?" he asked.

"Who're you?" Fargo questioned.

"Miss Bradbury's foreman," the man said.

"Looking for her and her pa," Fargo said.

The man was almost beside the Ovaro when he turned his head. "It's him. Get him," he yelled and Fargo saw the four figures rushing out from behind the main house, guns in their hands.

"Shit," he swore as he yanked the Colt from its holster as he reached down with his left hand and grabbed the man by the hair. He pulled the man against the pinto's side and jammed the muzzle of the Colt into his forehead as the man's eyes widened in fear and pain. He saw the others come to a stop at once. "Drop your guns or he'll need a new head," Fargo rasped.

"Jesus, do it," the man gurgled.

"They were here late last night. What'd they tell you?" Fargo demanded.

"That a crazy man was gunning for them and he'd be coming here looking for them. They took some things and hightailed it," the man said.

"What else?" Fargo asked.

"Miss Karen left orders to take care of the place

until she got in touch with me. She said they'd be back soon enough," the foreman said.

"They told you a pack of lies. I'm no crazy man and I don't have time to explain it now. You'll be hearing about it," Fargo said, still keeping the Colt pressed against the man's head. "Which way did they go?"

"South," the man said. Fargo flung him away and he fell sprawling on the ground. Fargo dug heels into the horse and raced away, crossed the nearest field when he spotted the two sets of hoofprints. They had stayed south, riding hard, the prints deep into the ground. After an hour they slowed, hoofprints no longer digging hard and he followed as they reached a narrow place on the bank of the Wabash. He followed his hunch that they had crossed at that spot and eased the Ovaro into the river. The current was lazy and he came out on the opposite bank almost across from where he'd entered the water.

He walked the horse along the bank and grunted in satisfaction as he found the hoofprints, deep in the soft soil of the riverbank. He swung the Ovaro after the tracks and saw where they rode up a hillside, onto a broad stretch of ground heavily sprinkled with shagbark hickory. He was into Missouri, that state filled with divided loyalties and twisted tensions. It was an appropriate place for them to flee, he grunted. The trail grew less clear but he was not the ordinary tracker and he followed it as they went through a forest of box elder.

He saw where they had stopped to rest and then gone on deeper into the forest. They were riding slowly now, tired or confident or both. When he emerged from the forest he drew to a halt as only one set of hoofprints met his searching gaze. He smiled. Karen had shown that she knew something about disguising a trail. Most trackers would have turned back and searched the forest again, certain they had missed seeing the double set of prints turn off someplace. But Fargo leaned low in the saddle, his eyes peering closely at the hoofprints and his smile was grudgingly appreciative. She had ridden behind her father, being careful to have her horse step almost exactly into the lead horse's tracks. But almost wasn't enough and he spotted the places where the second horse's hoofs spread too much, the edges no longer well defined.

The ruse had lost them a lot of time. It had taken careful, slow riding and he put the Ovaro into a canter as he followed the trail. It led into another forest, mostly white ash this time and the trail became a double set of prints again. They were sharp, not more than a few hours old and he kept the Ovaro at a canter. The forest trickled out, became a thin line of trees and he saw the hoofprints move down a slope and caught the flash of sun on a pond. He followed and saw where they had watered their horses and then gone on. They were riding leisurely now, he noted and he halted, dismounted, and pressed his fingers into the prints. The earth at the edges was warm but the center of each print was still cool, not yet warmed by the sun. They were only minutes ahead and Fargo put the Ovaro into a fast walk as he pulled the big Sharps from its saddle holster.

He crested a small rise, followed down a slope, and halted as he saw the two horses standing under a tall hickory. He slid from the saddle and moved down the slope on foot as Sam Bradbury came into sight. The man was drying his face with a towel and Fargo heard the rush of a stream. Karen appeared a few moments later rubbing her brown hair dry, her slender willow form encased in only a slip. She looked lovely, he noted with abstract rue as he stepped into the open, the rifle in his hands and aimed. "End of the road," he said.

Karen had halted alongside her father and both looked at him with complete shock on their faces. "You forget why you hired me, Sam?" Fargo asked.

"I guess so," the man said slowly.

"Damn you," Karen said. She stepped forward, pulled her shoulders back and her full breasts pressed tight against the smooth material of her slip. He remembered how delicately pink the tips had been. She read his thoughts at once. "Take me, to jail or to bed or both. Whatever you want, Fargo. But let him go. He didn't do anything. It was all my doing," she said.

"How about attempted murder?" Fargo said. "I think that's what Barnaby would call it."

"I'm not letting Karen spend her years in some filthy prison," Sam Bradbury said. "You'll have to kill me first."

"I don't want to do that," Fargo sighed.

"May I get dressed?" Karen asked and he nodded and she turned to where her skirt and shirt were lying on the ground. He watched her step into the skirt, long, slender legs another reminder. She reached down again, picked up the shirt and had it half on when she spun and he saw the six-gun in her hand, her finger tightening on the trigger.

"Aw, shit," he swore as he fired, his response automatic, dictated by the unswerving laws of survival.

"No," Sam Bradbury shouted hoarsely as he flung himself in front of Karen. Her shot slammed through him and he flew forward as the big Sharps exploded. The rifle's powerful bullet grazed his head as he fell and Fargo cursed again as Karen's chest erupted in a shower of red. "Goddamn, goddamn," he swore as he ran forward. She lay crumpled on the ground, the six-gun still in her hand, her nipples no longer a delicate pink, the light blue eyes only a dull echo, their flame extinguished.

He looked at Sam Bradbury. He lay dead. Karen's shot had torn through his heart from the back. Fargo turned away, walked to where he had left the Ovaro and put the rifle into its saddle holster. He returned to lay Karen across her saddle first, then Sam Bradbury on his mount. It was an unjust world, said the man. Maybe, Fargo wondered as he swung onto the Ovaro. Or maybe justice took its own ways and its own time, ignoring the rules mere humans tried to make. Maybe justice knew better than to trust the flawed instincts of men and women.

It's an unjust world, Sam Bradbury had said. But Fargo found himself thinking of other words he had learned as a boy. *I, saith the Lord . . . shall execute judgment and justice in the earth.* He moved the Ovaro forward. He sure as hell didn't have any better answer.

LOOKING FORWARD!

The following is the opening
section from the next novel in the exciting
Trailsman series from Signet:

THE TRAILSMAN #133
SAGE RIVER CONSPIRACY

*1860, New Dublin . . . in what
is now the state of Montana,
A town turned upside down,
where loyalty is betrayal,
and a man's face makes him a hero
or a corpse . . .*

There. He saw it again. A flicker of movement in the stand of yellow pine on the hillside. That made two of them, he thought. And if he had spotted two, there were probably a hundred. Blackfoot, creeping down the forested slope. Maybe more than a hundred.

Without reining in his Ovaro, the tall man turned in his saddle and glanced back at the supply train following him. Two dozen mule-drawn mountain wagons lumbered in the deep ruts cut through the bunch grass of the rolling plain, under low, sullen clouds. On the driver's seats were sharp-eyed men, surly, quiet, strange, hunched against the cold, stiff wind that blew out of the north into their faces. A dozen more men of the same kind rode beside the wagons. Sixty men all together.

Skye Fargo cursed inwardly. Why the hell had he taken this job anyway, leading this batch of toughs through bad Indian country? He turned back around in his saddle and rode a few more paces, glancing at the hillside again, reckoning chances.

Another movement. Subtle. But it was there. He sighed. The perfect spot for an ambush lay just ahead, where two gentle wooded slopes pinched the plains. The wagon train was heading for that narrow passage, and Fargo had no doubt that the trees on either side were swarming with armed Blackfoot.

Fargo turned and signaled one of the outriders to approach. The man rode up, a burly, bearded fellow. Fargo remembered his name was Willie. He was one of the few of these taciturn men whose name Fargo knew, even after three weeks on the trail. As far as he could make out, Willie seemed to be the foreman of the group.

"Indians in the trees," Fargo said quietly. Willie's brow darkened with questions but no fear. He nodded but didn't answer. "A lot of them," Fargo continued. "Pass the word back. On my signal, we'll circle and stand ready to fight."

Willie nodded again and fell back. Fargo slowed the pace of the train and glanced back from time to time. He hoped nothing would look suspicious to the watching Indians as the message was passed from man to man. If the Blackfoot suspected that they had been sighted, they would spring their ambush early, swooping down on the wagons as they rode strung out across the plain. Fargo watched as they drew nearer to the narrow passage. If they got too close to the gap . . .

Here goes, he said to himself as he suddenly put the spur to the Ovaro and turned him hard about. The first wagon followed, turning off the track and into the rough bunch grass. The driver laid his whip across the backs of the mules as they came around. In two minutes, the wagon train had doubled back and formed a tight circle, back ends facing out, mules teams angled to the inside, horses tethered inside the safety of the large inner circle. They'd lose fewer of their mounts this way than having them form part of the barrier. Also, the tight line of wagons would be harder for the Indians to breach.

Fargo rode about, giving orders. But the men seemed to know exactly what to do. They moved quickly and efficiently. Hell, they were lousy companions at the campfire, but they sure could ride a wagon train. Fargo hoped they'd also be good Indian fighters as he dismounted and tied the Ovaro. Willie approached with several of the other men.

"So, where's the redskins?" one red-haired man said roughly.

"They're out there." said Fargo, pointing. "Behind the trees. But they've lost the advantage of surprise. They're trying to decide if they can risk attacking us now that we've circled."

"I don't see none," said the redhead, craning his neck to peer at the slopes.

"Well then, why don't you walk over there and take a closer look?" Fargo said. "Then come back, minus your red scalp, and tell us what you saw."

The man shot an angry look at Fargo and stalked away.

"Just how long do we have to sit here, Fargo?" Willie asked.

"A few hours," Fargo said, glancing at the trees. "Maybe more. The Blackfoot are masters of the surprise attack. Right now they're pissed as hell that we spotted them. They'll wait until they think we've relaxed our guard. Or else they'll withdraw until we move on again."

"We're losing time," protested Willie. "We're supposed to be in New Dublin by nightfall." Several of the men nodded and muttered.

"Better late than never," said Fargo, walking away. Shit, he thought. Damn bunch of ingrates.

He paced around the inside of the circle of wagons watching the men. They were loading rifles, checking their ammunition, stropping their knife blades. None of them looked up as Fargo walked by, but he could feel their eyes on his back as he passed. A tough bunch, trail-hardened professionals, every last one of them. Fargo had seen the type before, but never in such a large group.

Why were these men all together on this wagon train? It was a question that had bothered him for three weeks on the trail from Denver City. Most of the wagon trains heading west were full of land-hungry men, wiry women, and silent children, settlers hoping to make a new life.

But these men were not settlers. They were loners. The type that were usually mountain men, prospectors, soldiers . . . or bandits. It didn't make sense.

Fargo sighed and climbed into one of the wagons. He settled himself onto bags of grain, propped open the canvas flap at the rear, and lay back to rest, keeping an eye on the slopes.

The chalky sky overhead was pressing downward, touching the tops of the bare bluffs in the distance. The cold, moist wind flapped the canvas. Snow wind, Fargo thought. There would be snow by morning. Nothing moved on the wooded hillsides.

Waiting, he thought. It was one of the most important skills for survival in the wild. Wait for the Indians to make a move. Wait for the deer to wander into the glade. Wait for your horse to whinny. Wait for darkness so no one can see you. Wait for a man to betray his thoughts in his words or in his face. Wait until you know exactly what's what. Then act.

Fargo smiled at his thoughts. Then why the hell hadn't he waited for a better offer? he asked himself. Shit. Three weeks back, he'd been at loose ends between jobs and sitting in a bar in Denver City when an Irishman with a lot of money asked him to do a job. Easy job. Take sixty men in a wagon train north to a place called New Dublin, right at the 49th parallel on the Canadian border. Half the money up front. The rest on arrival. Fargo had pocketed the first thousand dollars and set out.

But it had been a strange trip. Full of silences and questions with no answers. The men didn't talk to him. They fell silent when he approached their campfires. The wagons were full of supplies, food and ammunition. A lot of ammunition. Boxes of rifles and bullets and an entire wagon full of gunpowder. Fargo had asked Willie about that and about New Dublin. But Willie was buttoned up tight. And finally Fargo gave up questions and withdrew to his own fire, his own company. Now he was waiting. Waiting to find out what the hell was going on. Waiting for Blackfoot to attack.

Fargo sighed and stretched. Outside, he heard the clatter of pans. The cook was fixing the midday meal. He rose to make sure they weren't letting down their guard. The smell of bacon, coffee, and bread wafted inside the wagon and drew him out.

Most of the men were lined up at the campfire,

holding their tin plates for the cook to load up. Fargo checked the wagons. At least a dozen armed men were on guard, watching the plains and the hillsides beyond. Fargo joined the line at the fire and found himself behind Willie.

"No Indians yet," Fargo said, hoping to draw out the man. Willie glanced up and nodded. "By the way, what's your full name, Willie?" Fargo asked. "I never thought to ask."

"O'Brien," Willie muttered.

"Willie O'Brien," Fargo repeated, noting the bit of brogue in the man's accent. "Now, that's an Irish name if I ever heard one. How long have you been in America?"

Willie darted him a black look and turned his back. Fargo sighed and shrugged. Hopeless, he thought, as he took his plate of food and returned to the wagon. Now, what was taking those Blackfoot so long to make up their minds?

The attack came late in the afternoon, when the clouds had darkened from chalk to gray. Fargo had just climbed out of the wagon to stretch his legs when he caught sight of a long line of movement along the edge of the trees.

"This is it!" he shouted. "Take your positions and fire as soon as they're in range!" The men around him, many of whom were napping or playing cards, jumped to their feet and grabbed their rifles. Fargo checked his Colt and his Sharps rifle, touched the long knife strapped around his ankle, and vaulted onto the driver's seat and rolled into the wagon. He quickly pulled back the canvas for a better view. Two other men joined him, a skinny fellow and the redhead who had taunted him earlier.

"There're your Indians," Fargo said quietly, as he positioned the barrel of his Sharps on the top of the edge of the wagon and watched grimly as the Blackfoot emerged from the edges of the woods at the base of both hills. The redheaded man said nothing but pressed his lips tight, his squinting eyes watching the tribe.

"Oo-ee," said the skinny one, patting his long Lehman trade musket. "Got lots of targets for you." He moved the grain sacks and a barrel around to give himself better cover.

Fargo bent over and took a sighting on the approaching Blackfoot. The Indians rode forward in a long line, very slowly, not charging yet. They were still outside shooting range. Fargo's sharp eyes picked out the distinctive Blackfoot war bonnets with the feathers sticking straight up on their heads and ermine tails dangling on either side.

His lake blue eyes narrowed and swept the long line, estimating their number. Close to eighty. Sixty armed men from a fixed position against eighty attacking Indians had a sure chance of winning. Then his hopes sank. This was the first wave, he thought. It was an old Indian trick. Send in some of your force. Then, just when the battle is teetering and the paleface thinks he has a slender chance of winning, send in the rest, screaming bloody murder. It worked every time.

Just as the Blackfoot were within shooting range, one of the braves gave a yell and the line charged forward. Fargo took aim at a strong buck and squeezed the trigger. The Indian spun and fell, disappearing under the hooves of the oncoming horses. As Skye slipped another cartridge into the Sharps, the redhead got one. The skinny man missed and swore. Fargo heard rifle reports from the other wagons. Several more Indians dropped. The men were good shots, that was for sure. Maybe they had a chance of getting through this.

Fargo ducked as a shot zinged by his head and raised his rifle again, sighting an Indian in a war bonnet. He shot low, aiming for the belly, and the Indian slumped forward as the horse slowed and fell back into the oncoming line. Fargo slipped another cartridge into the rifle and then quickly drew his Colt.

As they neared, the Blackfoot suddenly turned and circled the wagons. Fargo watched as they passed, an endless blurred parade of bronzed and muscular warriors, whooping, braids flying, and rows of shell necklaces dancing against their chests. Their painted buffalo hide shields were strapped on their arms. Most had rifles. But the bows were no less deadly. Fargo popped up and shot two more in close succession. The redhead winged a third.

An arrow whizzed by and tore through the canvas. Several more struck with a thud against the wooden back of the wagon. A bullet ricocheted and Fargo heard a scream of agony. He glanced over to see the redhead grasping his side, blood oozing out between his fingers.

"Aw, shit," the skinny man said from behind him, reloading and squeezing off another shot. There was nothing either one of them could do, Fargo thought, as he turned his attention back to the Indians. A flash of pain burned his shoulder as an arrow whizzed by, grazing him. Fargo raised the Colt and shot a Blackfoot just as he was ready to let another arrow fly.

Out of the corner of his eye, he saw the redheaded

man struggling to sit up. As Fargo and the skinny one picked off more of the Indians, the dying man was painstakingly propping his rifle back up on the wooden wall. An Indian galloped by, leaning out from his saddle, rifle poised, searching for a target. The redhead pulled the trigger at the same moment the Indian fired on him. The rifles exploded simultaneously and Fargo saw the redhaired man jump once. He didn't move again. Fargo glanced out at the Indian, slumped across the back of his pony.

Fargo reloaded again and again, spending his fury on the Indians as they rode by. The skinny man inched up beside him and, pushing aside the dead man, ducked down behind the wooden boot. The skinny man was a good shot and a good soldier, Fargo thought. They timed their shots and reloadings so that one of them was shooting at any given moment.

There were many fewer Indians, Fargo noticed, and a lot of bodies lying on the plain. They rode farther from the train, their ranks thinned, dashing in for the sure shots.

"Wonder how many of our men are left?" Fargo muttered half to himself as he followed a moving Indian with his barrel and brought him down.

"We're all good fighters," the skinny man said, reloading and raising the rifle again. Fargo glanced over at him.

"Where'd you learn to fight?" Fargo asked idly.

The other man didn't look at him, but kept his eye on the Indians passing. They weren't shooting much, but were just circling.

"What are they waiting for?" the skinny man said, not answering Skye's question. Fargo sighed inwardly.

He wasn't going to find out anything from this one either.

"Seamuse to bring on the next trick," Fargo said. "My guess is those Blackfoot have more warriors still on the hillside. Or maybe they've got something else up those buckskin sleeves."

The answer came almost immediately, as a burning arrow tore through the canvas above their heads, setting the fabric on fire. So, the Blackfoot were going to smoke them out, Fargo thought. He pulled his neckerchief up over his nose and mouth, gesturing for the other man to do the same. They hunkered down and Fargo raised his Colt, catching a Blackfoot in the throat as he galloped close by. The brave grasped his throat with both hands as it spurted blood and slid from his mount.

The Indians redoubled their attack and between shots, Fargo kept an eye on the burning canvas. The Indians were bolder now, coming in closer. He ducked another arrow as it zinged by.

They could hold out for a while under the burning canvas. Usually, the canvas just burned right away, leaving the box of the wagon intact, still good cover. He wondered how far the fire was spreading, whether it had reached the supply wagons with boxes of rifles and . . .

"Goddamn gunpowder!" Fargo shouted from beneath his neckerchief.

"Shit!" the skinny man said, lurching sideways as a bullet whistled through.

"We can kiss it all good-bye if that blows!" Fargo said, reloading. "Cover me while I go check on it."

He swore and began sliding out onto the driver's

seat of the wagon, keeping low. He dropped onto the balls of his feet and ran, bent double.

Stray shots and arrows had wounded several of the mules and they brayed loudly. Inside the circle, no one was in sight. All the men had hidden in the wagons and were shooting. Half of the canvas-topped wagons blazed, the red-gold flames bright against the low gray clouds. Black smoke billowed skyward. None of the men had panicked and fled from the wagons, as settlers usually did when the canvas tops caught fire. The Indians counted on that. No, these men were professionals.

A burning piece of canvas had blown onto the grass in the center of the circle. It wasn't much of a fire yet, but Fargo could see it was spreading, and the steady wind would quickly sweep the narrow fire line across the grass circle, heading straight for the tall wooden-sided wagon which held dozens of barrels of gunpowder. He'd need help. Fargo bent down again and ran to one of the wagons that was not on fire. He lifted the canvas side. Five men were inside. One was Willie, who turned to reload. He started, seeing Fargo's face there, his neckerchief over his nose and mouth.

"What the hell?"

"Fire running toward the gunpowder," Fargo shouted. "I need three men to help me."

Willie and two men quickly jumped out. One man caught a stray shot in the calf, and another vaulted down to replace him, as the wounded one dragged himself back into the wagon.

"Come on!" Fargo shouted, removing his buckskin jacket. Willie and the two men did the same as they raced toward the open center of the circle. The greedy flames licked the tufts of dry grass and they burst into orange flame, then curled and charred black.

The men spread out in a line to face the oncoming fire. Fargo lifted the jacket above his head, advanced, and brought it down onto the burning grass, snuffing out the flames, beating the fire again and again as the black smoke choked him. He leapt aside as a stray arrow whizzed by, continuing to fight the fire. The men beside him beat back the flames as the wind blew stronger. Fargo fell back as the flames roared up again, their heat like a heavy wall. As the wind stiffened and blew the fire toward him, he felt his hair becoming singed and the skin on his face dry and cracked.

"Harder!" Fargo yelled. He glanced behind him and saw that the powder wagon was a dozen yards away. The mule team, still hitched to the wagon, was braying and struggling against their traces as the flames neared. There was a chance that the fire would pass under the wagon without igniting the gunpowder, but only if the flames moved fast enough not to catch fire to the wood or heat the powder to ignition. It was a slim chance. But the sweeping flames would cook the mules, he realized, as he continued to beat the flames. The fire was gaining, and the narrow band was spreading at the edges, threatening two other wagons and teams.

There was only one thing to do, he realized, but it was a big risk. Just then one of the men spun about and grabbed his shoulder, holding it tight. He staggered over beside one of the wagons. The Indians had sighted them in the center of the circle and were shooting between the wagons.